Kensington Quartet

Zulfikar Ghose

KENSINGTON QUARTET

A NOVEL

DALKEY ARCHIVE PRESS

McLean, IL / Dublin

Copyright © 2019 by ZulfikarG hose.
First edition, 2020.

All rights reserved.

CIP Data available upon request.

www.dalkeyarchive.com
McLean, IL / Dublin

Acknowledgements

A SENTENCE BY Peter Ackroyd in his biography of T. S. Eliot—'The sequence was now complete: although he had originally wanted to entitle it *Kensington Quartets*, in memory of his residence there, it was called *Four Quartets*'—released the imagery and produced the impetus to write a novel using Eliot's abandoned title, though what was for him plural must for me remain singular.

The formal conception of this novel with its rendering of memory as a structure of rhythms and partially reiterated themes of a reality that is experienced as inconclusive fragments and obsessive repetitions has involved incorporating phrases and lines from other writers, included in the text sometimes in italics and sometimes as an unacknowledged appropriation, which, originating in the work of Robert Browning, Donne, T. S. Eliot, Empson, Hardy, Hopkins, Keats, Shakespeare, Shelley, Wallace Stevens, James Thomson, Wyatt, Yeats, Virginia

Woolf, etc., and being familiar echoes within the universal English unconsciousness, no more need identification than when a painter appropriates the Mona Lisa or Las Meninas in a canvas upon which the vision represented is of another perception and another time.

Z. G.

The meeting with oneself is, at first, the meeting with one's own shadow. The shadow is a tight passage, a narrow door, whose painful constriction no one is spared who goes down to the deep well. . . . It is the world of water, where all life floats in suspension; where the realm of the sympathetic system, the soul of everything living, begins; where I am indivisibly this *and* that; where I experience the other in myself and the other-than-myself experiences me.

C. G. Jung, *Archetypes and the Collective Unconscious*

I

What might have been and what has been
Point to one end, which is always present.

T. S. Eliot, Four Quartets

I AM HERE now, just inside Kensington Gardens.

To the north the pebbled concrete expanse of the Broad Walk slopes up towards a pale blue sky above Bayswater. Two women with bundled-up toddlers and another pushing a pram, and farther up shadowy figures of three men in charcoal-grey coats, there is a scattering of ghostly bodies on the Broad Walk, the light so unusual, almost too bright, aglow in my mind, a surprisingly illuminated London. Glancing back in the direction of Palace Gate, I observe that you are striding up in that jaunty walk of yours, always so enthusiastically eager for the grass under the elms and a view of the Long Water. There are no shops to distract you, only consulates of foreign lands across the road you have no interest in, one displaying a flag, green and white, of indistinguishable nationality, hanging too limply. Your step always quickens in Palace Gate when the distant green blur of Kensington Gardens first catches your eye and even when the day is overcast and grey you see a sudden green shiver in the sky, for you it's the pulse of London, throbbing, as if it were your blood that surged with a sudden passion and made your breath come hard and loud—as that first time, that April, which then became the love-liest of months, when the first of English green you saw was here—all those prints of Constable's landscapes in the Blackie readers coming alive in the grass at your feet—and your blood bounded in amazement. Another three minutes and you will be coming into the Gardens, inflating your chest when you enter, as is your habit, taking a deep breath and holding it a long moment as when the doctor, his stethoscope's cold disc on your chest, says, *Breathe in and hold*, listening to your heart.

Past the congestion of cars on Kensington Road, I think I can see you among the pedestrians on the pave-ment, quite a crowd of them, though that is not unusual, you among them, momentarily lost but certainly there, I think I can see you, I know you are there, walking jauntily, your feet eager to step on grass, I know you are, you've always been, I don't even need to look. Not a day passes but you must come to what for you has been the heart of London, even when you're abroad you're always here, where your blood surges as if memory of this green were an infusion of a special oxygen for which you brain constantly craved.

You must have passed the other somewhere along Gloucester Road. He always stops to look into Karnac Books, to peer at the slim volumes, to touch a page or two, his eyes lingering upon a line where an incongru-ous, unexpected word strikes a note that rings a surpris-ing music, ravished too, his eyes by a phrase, a sudden revelation as if he saw a young woman stepping out of a bath, her naked foot glistening upon the white tile; or he stands a moment in front of the antique shop, arrested by glowing mahogany surfaces, and seeing a desk with a top of gold-tooled green leather imagines an eminent writer at his eternal composition who has just leaned back to weigh how well the recently written words are balanced; or you might have seen him looking fascinatedly at the display of fruit at the grocer's where his eye has been drawn to the pyramid of red apples which from a distance, in a moment's eruption of nostalgia for the tropics, it amused him to imagine were pomegranates.

A movement among some pigeons in front of the entrance to the Flower Walk distracts me. The little wrought-iron gate is only partially open, a nice suggestion of an entrance to a private garden, to its right the little fountain with its bronze dog in a tail-wagging pose, three pigeons pecking at the ground on the fountain's circular periphery. When was the fountain erected, he never saw it, you never noticed it, but of course there are so many things that have always been there though observed by God knows no one, and he had his own favourite things to look at in the Flower Walk, and you too always seeking reassurance that yesterday and tomorrow had a presence in the objects before you, you could see summer blossoms even in the winter's twigs in the Flower Walk. What flowers can there be now? It's a mild morning in mid-October, the sky so blue with small rose-tinged satin clouds and the sun so unseasonably warm, one expects hyacinths to be in bloom. This is not the weather one associates with England. Instead of a drizzle, a beautiful glow descends upon the park, pale yellow light raining down from heaven as if cherubs sat cushioned upon the luxurious clouds and strew petals of sweet jasmine upon the earth. There is no blustery autumnal wind, instead a stillness of air, one's breath held as when confronted by a surprising vision—as during a casual stroll through the National Gallery among familiar landscapes, one's eye is suddenly caught by a previously unperceived diffusion of light in a well-known Old Master and is so shocked to see a visionary dimension in the perspective that one's belief in the fixedness of certain surfaces is confounded. I go towards the Flower Walk and just before entering look quickly to the right to see if you have reached the top of Palace Gate. A 49 bus is waiting to turn right to go down Gloucester Road and two other buses are proceeding east towards Albert Hall. You must be some- where behind the wall of buses.

He, as usual, has probably not come up to Palace Gate but turning left at Victoria Grove has entered Launceston Place to saunter back and forth past the houses, com- paring each one with its neighbour, looking for unique details in a row of basically identical houses, determining which one is the best, recording in his mind the location of the one with a wrought-iron trellis for climbing roses framing the large ground-floor window together with the image of a plump ginger cat contentedly asleep in the turned-up flower bed below the window, for that is the house he will buy one day when he is wealthy, or so he dreams, always going on a detour from Gloucester Road on his way to Kensington Gardens, one little bifurcation in the labyrinth of the future which leads nowhere and from which he must retreat each time and come up to Kensington Road via De Vere Gardens, projecting in his mind a future when the garden is in full summer bloom and the cat looking up at the butterflies attracted to the violet flowers on the small buddleia tree in the corner of the garden and himself at the door, entering his house. It's a perfect house, he has decided, in this little hidden away corner, Launceston Place, which with its prettily trimmed front gardens is like a street in a Sussex village, he will be happy here, standing there behind the drawing room window, glass of Scotch in hand, watching the ginger cat, which will be named Perdita, taking a leap at a butterfly and missing it, that will be his home, in this quiet little street close to Kensington Gardens.

Two young gardeners in green T-shirts and moss-green trousers are raking the soil of a flower-bed. One is male, the other female, but both with short-cropped blond hair. Their faces and arms are sunburned, their skin suffused with the accumulated light of the late Indian summer when for nearly a fortnight a hot brightness has filled the Gardens and the shortening days have seemed as long as in midsummer. When I see the two gardeners go past each other in opposite directions there is, for a moment, one indistinguishable mass of their combined being, one behind the other, from which suddenly emerge two bodies and I realise that my eyes following what they believe to be the shape of the girl are deceived, it is the boy I am looking at, but when I discern the shape of the boy in the other I conclude that I was not mistaken, I was indeed looking at the girl, but then I have to work it out all over again because the figure I was so convinced was the male's is in fact the girl. And in that moment when the two seemed one, my already knowing that they were in fact two I saw as a third the combination of the two as one, and then when they are again separate and are two I continue to see the other one who came into a moment's illusory being as the third.

There are, always, three of us. As in the French lesson with Mr Little glaring out at the class from behind his desk, slapping the air with his hand, beating time while the boys chanted *Je suis, Tu es, Il est* at the top of their voices, *I am, You are, He is, Je suis, Tu es, Il est*, again and again, in that classroom chorus in which I imagine you still hear his voice.

Mr Little kept a bag of sweets on his desk and when a boy answered a question correctly he would take a sweet and, like a fielder aiming a ball at the wicket-keeper's gloves, throw it hard at the boy, who was expected to catch it but sometimes got hit on the head instead. Mr Little was an Englishman and once when a boy answered,

'Oui, Monsieur Petit', he banged his fist on the desk and shouted, 'Non, non! Appelez-moi Monsieur Leetle, s'il vous plaît!' As sometimes happens with men whose name indicates a physical attribute, his body was the opposite of what was signified by the name; and precisely because he was very large, over six feet tall and very wide at the waist, and not because he was named Mr Little—for the principle governing the invention of nicknames by schoolboys is not wit but irony—the boys called him Old Tiny. His black gown flecked with chalk dust, the white collar of his shirt curled and brown at the edges and his loosely knotted greasy grey tie giving him the aspect of a disreputable old actor suspected of having downed two or three large whiskies before coming on the stage, Old Tiny would interrupt a boy's squeaky and stumbling recitation of some lines from Racine and in a bellowing voice declaim twenty lines from *Andromache*, spit flying out of his mouth, that startled the boys into an astonished silence in which they obscurely understood that the drama was not in the meaning of the words as much as in the vocal force composed of rhythm and volume emanating from a human throat for which the words were a cue prompting the brain to commence some primeval cry, and in that sudden explosion of language was a previously unheard music that produced in one's mind a spiritual shock.

Think of it for your screenplay, you said to Stannie, nothing but a large head filling up the entire black-and-white screen in a delirium of declamation, the mouth opening and closing rapidly, the tongue, the teeth, the spittle on the lips, and words, words, words flying out of the agitated throat, too rapid for grammatical coherence, and then, keep the mouth open, freeze the image, no sound, hold the silence, time stopped now, all senses suspended, collapsed in a pathetic heap the mechanistic universe, but what meaning then, what music! It was in the Drayton Arms. There, or in the Goat, or the Duke of Clarence. When most you could afford were two half pints. Stannie looked at you doubtfully, always his first impulse at any of your suggestions, always suspicious you might not be serious but building up towards some joke. But when he saw that you were being neither ironical nor flippant, he said, Perhaps in some obscure guttural tongue, a language God might use to scold humanity. Words painful to hear, you said, but once heard, beautiful their after-sound. Stannie nodded his head thoughtfully, staring into the half-pint his hand had just raised to his mouth, but looked up startled when you added, Like a memory of orgasm, and wondered whether you'd not meant to be flippant from the start, but then, perhaps, there was no irony to it, none.

The sky so blue, the air so clear, everything is far away and right in front of my nose at the same time, it's an elastic universe, the horizon stretches out into farthest space and snaps right back to my eyelids, as if I am again in that April when Yuri Gagarin orbited the earth and from the apogee saw the green specks of parks and heaths encircling London or that February in John Glenn's *Friendship 7* orbiting thrice the world so blue, so clear, seeing everything at a glance, and then when I come down to earth, like the astronaut in his craft splashing down by the Bahamas, blink hard to shake off the momentary disorientation to see where I am, I am here, in Kensington Gardens.

From the Flower Walk I cannot see if the 49 bus has entered Palace Gate, which it must have done by now, surely. Probably reached Cromwell Road by now. You know the route, stop by stop, all the way to Clapham Junction, you'd moved there for a time but returned almost daily, on the 49, to Kensington. A short walk from Clapham Junction to your room in the street behind the cemetery. The surprise, each time, waking on some mornings to the voice of a priest at a grave side ceremony, and, looking out from the first-floor window, within banks of mist swirling among the chestnut trees the shock of seeing the ghostly appearance of the mourners. And on some mornings the sound of a spade hitting the turf, stirring in one's sleep a memory of turning up the earth for a planting.

It would be more efficient to use a tractor, you said, but there is something comforting observing a solitary man digging the ground, as if the scene were a fragment from a pastoral past which evoked a buried memory of one's roots that persuaded one to believe that to be received in the ground thus prepared by a peasant's labour was a beautiful fate, something the living must envy, for another human had turned the earth for you, not a machine, had cared for you with his hands, and in the bowl of his hands as if he gently held in it a small white dove lifted up your soul.

Now this is very strange, you said to Stannie, sitting in the Goat. You said the dead were being ravished. So unbearable the desire of the living who had exhausted the hallucinogenic potential of mushroom or flower that they sought to experiment with the dead. You said you heard music played from the bones of the dead. It must have been the November wind blowing through the leafless chestnut trees. How can one explain desire so unbearable? You said that semen spilled into the eye-sockets of skulls. It had nothing to do with magic or with the deeds of the superstitious. You were convinced you witnessed the living. You saw a man's buttocks rising from a grave. A woman with flowing black hair played a long, exuberant air on a flute, but there was no melody, only a shriek. Shaven-headed men stomped the ground at the top of the grave from where the buttocks rose and fell. There was a whooping cry and the clapping of hands. Then the yell of the man pierced by orgasm. The flute shrieked. You were not dreaming, and nor had you regressed to some former life where such acts were a periodic tribal ceremony, for just then you heard a plane descending over London, following the course of the river, you imagined, in its approach to Heathrow, and you knew from the sound of its engines it was a turbo-prop, a Vanguard, British European Airways.

Stannie did not believe any of that. This is London, he said, not bloody Bombay. The City of Dreadful Night, you said, and declaimed, *As I came through the desert thus it was, As I came through the desert . . .* which prompted Stannie's memory of the stanza you both knew by heart and he too in a jolly merriment of recitation declaimed, *Eyes of fire Glared at me throbbing with a starved desire,* but as if already struck by the terror of the lines which followed he stopped and stared at you in disbelief, suddenly glimpsing that you spoke true, while you continued, *The hoarse and heavy and carnivorous breath Was hot upon me from deep jaws of death.* Bloody hell, Stannie said, still staring in disbelief, seeing that a nineteenth-century poet of dipsomaniacal visions had been perfectly sober after all, for the symbols discovered by a mind within the depth of its despair prefigured a literal truth, bloody hell, Stannie said, the intoxication in that case, mate, is in the poetry, and we're a pack of superstitious pagans howling in the night, but I still don't believe it, he said, not fucking likely, you must've been fucking dreaming, he said, but you had him staring with a worried look again when you retorted, What about the carnivorous fucking breath, then, and then you made a joke of it, saying, Poets and graves are the same thing and one of them is called Robert, that made Stannie laugh and go fetch two more halves of bitter.

The male gardener has placed the long pole of his rake

across his shoulders and holds it there with his wrists, the two hands hanging limply in front. He stands with his head tilted and watches the girl who is kneeling on the ground with her hands in the earth pulling at a broken root. Perhaps there is nothing there for her to extract and she has some other reason to keep her hands thrust into the soil.

It was not a trick of light, you said, taking the half-pint away from your mouth, though the mist that morning was thick and the figures recalled to your mind the phrase *the ghostly paradigm of things*, inevitably, you thought, as you said to Stannie when he looked at you with fixed eyes, gravely suspicious, as if a leak had sprung up at the back of your skull, sitting in the Goat, taking your time over your half because Stannie and you could afford only two rounds. What, he finally asked, a hairy arse bobbing out of a grave, someone doing it to a bloody corpse? And when you answered, I imagine it must be bloodless, Stannie jerked his head back, suggesting he did not think the joke funny. The odd thing was, you said, maintaining what you had envisioned was true, I was filled with a sense of beauty. Not by what I saw but by the fact that I was seeing. That awareness of the thing itself. Really very extraordinary. The mist dispersing, yes, quite extraordinary, the patchy, shifting light obliging one to keep one's eyes open so as not to be deluded by a sudden rearrangement of light and dark and seeing something that wasn't there. Now Stannie laughed and said, Bugger off! You were not so easily to be dismissed and quickly responded, I mean like when one hears Mozart's *Requiem*, there's the feeling of being saturated by the beauty of the thing, that inner light. Stannie, gravely suspicious again, looked at you with narrowed eyes, raised his glass and took a sip, and said mockingly, That illumination of the bleeding soul, perhaps? You were not going to let his empiricist's weariness with extra-sensory matter mock you out of your conviction. No, no, you said, nothing mystical about it, but just the shock, like when you see one of those dark pictures by Goya depicting the appalling misery of a human face staring at the firing squad and you become overwhelmed by beauty in that deadly, still moment— and where is timelessness experienced but within the soul?—when opposites complement each other and eliminate contradiction and you recognize that beauty is the face of death. Stannie drank from his glass and put it down. You're not going to start on the bleeding inexpressible again, are you? he asked. Listen, you said, like one imparting an important message, beauty is death, and death beauty, and, of course, Stannie quickly added in an ironical voice, That is all ye know on earth, and all ye need to know, nodding his head emphatically on the stressed syllables:

all   know   earth   /   all   need   know

But if his choice of an ironical tone had been influenced by a desire to dismiss the images presumed to be an affront to a rational mind, Stannie, even as he spoke aloud the words *need to know*, had a vision of his own, he admitted, and told the story, when finding himself confused by banks of mist while driving once across Bodmin Moor and having to come out of his car when he thought he had slid off the road he heard a human voice yell out some primaeval cry as if about to be stabbed in the heart and, looking to his right, saw atop an eminence a man, starkly silhouetted against a wall of grey-white mist floating past behind him, stretch out his arms and cry out once more, roaring this time, and then, bringing his arms down as if he embraced a woman, commence what appeared to be an eagerly executed waltz, and as he swung round Stannie observed that he was naked. You could see, sitting in the Goat, sipping your beer, that Stannie's eyes had become worried, for appearances were not to be trusted, it almost hurt an Englishman to have to admit that the cause-and-effect Newtonian edifice perhaps was not that stable, even stone was made of grains of sand, and if there was an empirical resolution that shaped events, there was also the need to placate secret superstitions, as when going to a Christian service in a great cathedral one looks up at the sun catching a spot on the magnificent stained-glass window and instead of seeing the figure of a familiar saint kneeling by a rock one sees, with a strong inner sense of satisfaction, some need in that inner self being in that moment fulfilled, a satyr in conjugal possession of a woman, his eyes leering. Then Stannie spoke, in the morose way he had when obliged to make a reluctant admission: We do not know what we can believe but must have something to believe in, and silent for a moment, swirling his beer, looking into his glass, not drinking, then added, glancing up at you, that's why God is such a bleeding success. But that's not what you'd been talking about, you were about to tell him but did not, avoiding what you hoped was self-evident, and remarked instead, Orgasm as the mystical apprehension of death, isn't that what the ancient poets meant, the virgin who kills her living body by entering a nunnery is she not penetrated by the love of Christ, the young men killed in the great wars, were they not designated the glorious dead who thus acquired an everlasting beauty, and in Piccasso isn't the horror of Guernica more beautiful than his paintings of harlequins and guitars, and when Lear comes howling to the stage with the dead Cordelia in his arms are we not driven to tears by the nearly unendurable beauty of the scene? Ah, my friend, you wanted to say, too, but did not, there's a terrible cruelty in our visions of beauty, because before you could utter the words you heard Stannie begin to murmur the familiar quotation, *A terrible beauty* . . . hearing which, you joined his voice with yours to complete the phrase, . . . *is born*. And you saw Stannie stare at you with terror in his eyes, though you realised later that it was not terror but that suddenly coming into sharp focus of a revelation that the eyes find themselves staring at amazedly, and there was a palpitation within you, too, which must have sprung a mask across your face as if in that moment you were one in a Greek chorus and had to chant out the horror just discovered confirming the birth of beauty in circumstances of the most appalling barbarity. You drained the little remaining beer and left the Goat, Stannie pulling up the collar of his charcoal grey coat and you plunging your hands into the pockets of your old tweed coat as the two of you stepped out into High Street, Ken, which was throbbing and ticking with a scarcely moving mass of cars, buses and taxis though it was well past the rush hour and night had fallen. You know, you said, keeping close to Stannie on the crowded pavement, walking to De Vere Gardens, every time I come out of the Goat I remember that I've once again forgotten to ask the landlord if the pub was named after a famous novelist who grew up here as a young girl, Virginia Stephens was her name. To Stannie's questioning look you answered, She was nick-named Goat and used to play there, you raised a hand and pointed a finger across the road to Kensington Gardens. You mean Virginia . . . but before Stannie could get in the surname, you said, The very same, referred to by the beady-eyed Ezra Pound rather nastily, but as always with Pound, not without literal precision, as *the feeble-minded Woolf female*.

I proceed along the Flower Walk, going past the young gardeners. The girl is still bent over the earth with her knees on the ground and her hands thrust into the soil. The male has positioned himself opposite her and has also put his hands into the soil. To do so, he has cast his rake aside and dropped himself to the ground, falling on his knees, and is bent over the earth exactly as she is. Their heads are very nearly touching. The soil must be very loose, so easy it has been for them to thrust their hands into it well past the wrists. I do not know what it is that they are searching. They are saying something to each other but I've walked away too far to be able to catch the words. Perhaps it's only a game, finding and holding each other's hands where they can't be seen in the dark earth, the fingers meeting like blind worms, finding each other through feeling, blind as love, one climbing above another, becoming entwined. I walk on. The last thing I see is a gleaming line on the girl's neck where the light catches the moisture on her skin.

Blue and purple pansies are blooming in a flower-bed. A squirrel springs out of the darkness of the bushes at the back, races towards me, stops among the pansies and stands up on its hind legs, and, seeing that I continue to walk past, offering it nothing, hops back and goes scampering into the darkness. The wooden bench just past the first of the two palm trees is unoccupied and I stand before it a moment but decide not to sit down. There's a plaque fixed to the top of the bench. IN MEMORY OF. Always in memory of someone. WHO LOVED AND CARED FOR THE BIRDS

HERE. Kind soul, walking up and down the Flower Walk, broadcasting seed. A pigeon eyes me from the flower-bed. But the man who loved and cared is a ghost in the unoccupied bench. Looking from there at the palm tree, and mentally excluding the large bare trees in the background, seeing only the vivid green fronds of the palm against the blue sky, I am reminded of a similar perspective in a tropical land, in a desert climate, but I turn around quickly and as I proceed towards the second palm tree my eye catches the red streak of the London double-deckers on Kensington Road. That 49 bus must be caught in the traffic bottleneck at South Ken. Always a mess there, at South Ken, by the tube station. The 14 bus to Putney and the 30 to Roehampton also in the bottleneck. The first bus you knew in London was the 30. The request stop near Drayton Gardens on Old Brompton Road. Your first residence in London. Drayton Gardens, named after a poet who had been forgotten. Nice pub, the Drayton Arms, near the bus stop, where you will sometimes sit for an hour with Stannie, sipping from a half-pint, tossing ideas, heads-you'll-use-it, tails-you-won't, and sketching images for the concatenation of random shots for his screenplay. You took the same bus, the 30, to Roehampton on Saturdays to go to the school's cricket ground and open the innings. If the number plate on the bus had a nought in it, it was bad luck, you had better be on guard against getting a duck, but if it contained a nine you were going

to be in form, the runs were going to flow. God knows
how you'd arrived at that formula or whence came this
superstition of numbers as a persistent memory in your
blood but your life was ruined when you saw a nought
in the number plate when the bus turned up, no one
knew but you knew, you'd better be on guard even if
what was going to happen had to happen. Sometimes
you were out without scoring and during the miserable
walk back to the pavilion you remembered the nought
on the number plate and knew that this destiny had
been foretold, there was nothing you could have done
about it, still it was a miserable thing to be made an
outcast, to know it had been decided beforehand the
umpire's finger would go up before you'd scored a run
and banish you from the lovely green square. Sometimes
in your misery you resisted the role of one trapped in a
predetermined plot. It had been a coincidence. What had
the randomness of numbers on a bus to do with your
performance as a cricketer? If it had rained all afternoon
and there had been no play, the number you saw on
the bus would have proved irrelevant. But that was how
fate worked, giving you some reason to think it had
nothing to do with you, you were a free agent, only to
strangle you a little more tightly in its grasp. A sports-
man's superstitions. Always looking for signs to con-
firm future fertility, to make a big score, always going
in dread of an unfavourable prophecy, knowing there's
no deity who's not gleefully malicious, hysterical with

belly-shaking laughter when he's fucked you up again.
Nice the chance that had you living in a street named
after a poet but, should you identify with him, unfortu-
nate the circumstance that he's no longer read. What did
Drayton write that he be forgotten? O the trees and seasons, no doubt, his mistress fair, no doubt, remembrance
of things past, no doubt, in time which is always present,
the living and the dead, no doubt. A lovely green, the
fanned leaves of the palm tree, as in an oasis in some
desert, such a surprise here in Kensington Gardens on
a day in October, however fair. But then in the foreign
lands you always carried a small short-wave radio in your
pocket and sitting in a park, on a bench with a row of
palm trees behind it, you held the little Grundig by your
ear and listened for the time signal from Greenwich.
Always connected to London. Big Ben before the BBC
news, the World Service, Big Ben striking nine while
you sat listening intently in another time zone.

A little further up the Flower Walk is a second palm
tree and roughly equidistant from the two trees is a
double bench set back from the Walk with a little path
leading to it. Everything symmetrical in the gardener's
plan, clean and logical perspectives, neat arrangements,
the argument of design. A woman sits on the bench, her
right leg crossed over the left, blue jeans, black shoes,
brown leather jacket buttoned up over a blue polo-neck,
head bent, reading a book, but the head is swaying gently, her ears are plugged with ear-phones with wires going

down into a pocket, she's reading and hearing music, some sweet oldie or some screaming rock or some rapid unintelligible hip hop or some adagio for strings perhaps, some cadenza, some intermezzo, some music she has heard before and now lets it flow into her ears as some sort of continuous affirmation of a secret belief without needing to think about it while reading a book.

Past the second palm tree in the Flower Walk there is another flower bed where the soil has been turned up and there are shadows on it of twisted and intertwined lines from the bare branches of a weeping birch that arches over the Walk like a tent stripped bare of its canvas. A young mother has placed her little boy, a two-year-old bundled up for a winter's day, though it's not winter and, indeed, too warm for autumn, in the flower bed where the tree's quivering shadows throw a camouflage pattern on his quilted jump suit, and is taking a picture of him with a small camera. The boy raises his arm. He looks like a miniature astronaut in his little down jump suit with its hood drawn tightly over his head. He's waving at the earth. Hello and goodbye. I imagine him looking at the picture when he's sixty, or at some earlier time, when he's twenty-two and has gone home from the university for the long vacation, and his mother says, 'Look, Jeremy, what I found, a picture of you when you were not quite two', and he stares amusedly at the baby astronaut while his mother recalls an anecdote from his infancy which he has heard before, for it has become part of the family's lore, but he has never been able to recall the event of which he was the admired central figure when everyone thought him so precocious, so gifted, but at sixty he will be alone in his study, counting the years to his retirement from the bank, looking through some old papers, mostly bills kept in case the paid-for work proved unsatisfactory and then forgotten long after the warranted time had run out, and coming across the pocked and faded print, recalling what his mother had said when he was twenty-two about the time when he was not quite two, he will resolve to have the picture restored and an enlargement made for his thirty-two-year-old daughter Doris who takes such a keen interest in the family history, keeping everyone's memory alive.

There are shadows here from the leafless trees, the air feels cold. The sun is shining on the bandstand and on the Round Pond. Must be warmer out there, away from this gloom. This world of cobwebs. Invisible threads you suddenly smash into that stick to your forehead as if they'd oozed out of your head. I come out of the Flower Walk and follow a path to the bandstand. Under the sun now. Certainly a bit warmer. Who's that, then, can it be him? I can't believe it can be him walking out from behind the bandstand. I've been watching out for him, how could he have slipped past, gone a long way around to come out from behind the bandstand? I have to laugh, for the figure I'm looking at is a woman. I first saw her in silhouette, slim and tall, and was confused, not confused

but persuaded to transform to another the distant outline of one not yet fully drawn in my mind, so that for
a moment the outline took on a shape already there and
my imagination insisted that a preconceived idea, more
a fancy than an idea, was a true perception. In fact, he
is nowhere here, nowhere to be seen. Perhaps he was not
coming to the Gardens but going to the library in the
High Street. Or perhaps he was on his way to the Goat
to meet Stannie. Or only going to Launceston Place to
look at his chosen house, to feel the thrill of rehearsing a
secure, opulent future. There are other people and children on the crisscrossing paths. When I look towards the
Round Pond I see only silhouettes and when towards the
Serpentine Gallery I see green and blue coats and other
colours of scarves and boots and eyes and noses and lips.
In one direction the light is blinding and I can't see a
thing. Perspectives keep changing, of course; so many of
the trees have been cut down. The library is no longer
in the High Street. It's a bank now, a branch of a foreign
bank, with signs in Arabic, symbols of currencies. Men
sit at computer terminals and type columns of numbers and write a coded correspondence in Arabic in the
room where you consulted an encyclopaedia to look up
facts about Thomas Addison and found yourself reading
about Aristotle and then went eagerly to the Philosophy
section on the ground floor. You pulled out the book,
turned to the first page. *All men by nature have a desire
to know.*

A bank now, the library, you went in and out that door, carrying borrowed books. Whole systems of thought under your arm. Signs and symbols of currencies. But the bank will have gone the next time you visit, its rooms empty, only an estate agent's board outside—FOR SALE and below that announcement the words, ALL ENQUIRIES, and a phone number—they will have taken away all the money, all the books, constructed vaults and shelves elsewhere. But even when abroad you've only to remember the building and you see the white-framed windows on the red brick, the bay window above the ornate front door, the clock tower crowned by a cupola, and there's an echo as if the words had been transformed to particles of dust in the empty vaults and rooms and a sudden gust caused by an unexpected draft sent them drifting in the air, little dust devils of knowledge spiralling in the emptiness. All men by nature. Tornadoes of words that sent your brain spinning and tumbling under a loud roar of ideas, words, words, words, amazement still in thy thalamus sits. Have a desire to know. Not all men, though; some are content to count money, sitting there at the greasy till, in that same corner where you came to the shelf and found Aristotle, fingers flicking through foreign currencies, heads full of conversion rates, nothing to them but a laughable irrelevance your rage for order, perfectly solid and secure in the vault their bars of gold, the books are gone, a bank now, the library, and soon, on the next visit, empty space for sale, a real estate speculation, with a phone number for all enquiries.

I try to imagine the elm trees that I took for granted in the past, for which very reason I did not see them then and therefore do not see them now but know, only know, they were here, perhaps there was one with the vast girth of its trunk right here, right in front of my face, my nose almost touching the bark, blocking out everything in my view, but now it is empty space I can walk through. I was abroad when Dutch elm disease struck the trees, absent from London for a long time, and did not see them being cut down; if I had witnessed the workers with the chain-saws I would not be able to walk here without seeing the trees falling when the chain-saw cut through the trunk, for that association would spring up from my memory each time, I would not be able to enter the Gardens without the unbearable shriek of the chainsaw when it is in the fleshiest part of the trunk piercing my ears. But then, because I know that is what happened when I was not here, I am compelled to be a vicarious witness, a speculator in images who must transform remembered newspaper information into its probable appearance, find myself in a posthumous world, and even as I feel relieved that my ears are not assailed by the shriek of the chainsaw, even in that moment arrows slam into my ears and a horrible shrieking splits my brain. I see nothing. I hear nothing. I am still abroad. It is because there is so much light reflecting from the surface

of the Round Pond that when I look in that direction
the people appear as silhouettes. I decide to walk the
other way, towards the Serpentine Gallery. There was no
Serpentine Gallery then as there are no elm trees now,
but the building was there and looked different because
it served some other purpose than as an art gallery, just
as certain perspectives in which the elms were a conspicuous detail are now altered although the vanished elms
still have a remembered presence for those who saw them
before they were cut down: all absent things remain present, your memory rings in a tree-trunk with a record of
each year's sunshine and rainfall and that one exceptionally hot summer indelibly marked in the core.

You never cared for the Round Pond. Only children
there with little boats; sometimes an older man with a
beautifully crafted little yacht which he has made with his
own hands, the sharp-edged hull of polished teak shining
brightly even on a grey day; always anxious women there,
mothers watching their children, or the woman with the
man, anxious that he not be disappointed with what he
has made, otherwise he will be in a surly mood the rest
of the day. You never lingered by the Round Pond. You
looked at it from a distance, sometimes came close to
the shore on windy days to see the little waves create
the semblance of an oceanic storm for the little boats
and the little sailor-children running up and down the
edge of the Pond like the crew on a liner, but you never
lingered there, you strode on, even on windy days.

Though sitting in the Goat one evening, the first draft of Stannie's screenplay the subject of discussion, you said, Put in a scene of little Virginia in a white frock with navy blue bands at the cuffs and the V-neck collar edged with pleated ruffles running excitedly on the edge of the Round Pond shrieking with delight seeing the little waves thrown up by the wind. Stannie gave you an uncomprehending glance and said, Whatever for? It won't take half a minute, you answered, just a quick shot of a girl excited to see the waves. But why? demanded Stannie, and you, rising from your chair, said, Drink up, my turn, but did not speak aloud the phrase in her Diary which you'd remembered, *& time shall be obliterated*, which perhaps was why.

I realise I have taken a path going away from the Serpentine Gallery and am walking towards Peter Pan. There are rowers on the Long Water. They slip through the shadows cast by the trees on the water's edge. One rows energetically past and disappears under the bridge, making for the Serpentine. In that quick glimpse I had of him, I thought he wore a brown suit with a double-breasted jacket. He always wears that brown suit, even when he goes rowing on the Serpentine. It's too far for me to run up to the bridge to see who the rower is when he emerges from under the bridge on the other side. I am nearly certain I recognized the brown suit, the one he had had made at Barker's, but then, as I come closer to the shore of Long Water, I observe that another rower, who has a young woman sitting opposite him and who I thought was wearing a dark blue short coat is in fact wearing a grey jacket, and so it is possible that that brown suit was some other colour, perhaps a shade of burgundy. The light is extraordinary today. It is quite unbelievable. I see something and then can't believe I saw it. The other rower, with the woman sitting opposite him, has pulled his boat towards the farther shore and guides it to a spot under overhanging willow branches that form a little alcove. The woman stands up and, like one balancing on a tight rope, steps gingerly towards him. He slides to his left on his buttocks to make room for her when she reaches the wide board on which he is seated; she turns around, her red tartan skirt swinging about her knees, and sits down, and for a few moments the boat rocks. Even before the boat has stopped rocking, the man and the woman have flung their arms around each other and she has raised her face to his, her eyes closed and lips parted. If it were summer the willow branches would draw a green curtain in front of the lovers and even now, if I had not seen them rowing to the water's edge, their presence there would have gone unremarked, for the leafless branches do make for some obscurity, but because I have seen them enter that darker area and can continue to distinguish the surface impressions precisely, which to another looking by chance in that direction for the first time might appear to be some abstract motion, I can therefore see that the man's lips are now pressed hard against the woman's and that his hand has quickly unfastened the three or four top buttons of her green woollen cardigan and has disappeared behind it. I hear a yell to my left and look away. It is a boy of four or five dressed in a carnival costume with a silver cardboard crown on his head brandishing a wooden sword and running around a tree. The costume is that of a priest. He has cut all the evil of the world to pieces with his sword. The cardboard crown covered with aluminium foil is his prize. He is the new monarch of the world. The priest who would be king. God's ruler. The boy yells again. God's true word for the people. I look back towards the distant shore. It seems to have suddenly darkened under the willow branches. I know there's a couple making love there but if I had not seen them earlier I'd swear there was no one there. Only a boat abandoned there on the water's edge. Then the water seems to swell and send out a gentle wave and then another, slightly higher wave; soon the water becomes considerably agitated and the boat seems caught in a storm.

The willow's bare branches thrash in the wind. There is no boat there, there could not be. You were assembling like a tentative archaeologist fragments—the images on some startlingly perfect shards after all these years, on some pieces of glass or clay weathered into blurry vagueness—picked up on the shore to form perhaps an urn, perhaps a vase, something once whole and beautiful. There could not be a boat there. A barrier on the

Serpentine side of the bridge prevents rowers from entering the Long Water. It was not so when the elms were
alive. You rowed into the Long Water then hoping no
one else had already occupied the little curtained area
behind the willow's branches. You could tell from the
stillness of the water that you were lucky. Not quite
red, but scarlet, the tartan skirt, for a moment swinging
above her knees, not a green cardigan with buttons but
a V-necked sweater, navy blue angora, soft where your
finger-tips probed the V. Not this delusion, but reality,
warm as living flesh, a gyration of forms swarming in the
air like gnats above the water's surface, not delusional
this rash of presences, the flash of dark eyes when spots
of sunlight pierce the willow branches, your finger-tips
throbbing.

I start in the direction of the bridge but cannot walk
towards it. Something has gone wrong. I had wanted to
stand on the bridge and look down upon the Serpentine
and watch the rowers and look beyond the distant trees
towards St James's. I had wanted to walk across Hyde
Park. There are trees there I have known for forty years.
There is one with a trunk so wide there is a cavity at
its base that has room for two chairs where he sat one
evening with a woman while the wind outside snapped
the branches and thrushes sang their sunset songs. Inside
the tree, he held her. She caressed his thigh. The sap
stirred. A gust of wind and the branches broke into a
dance, the thrushes went silent. This is the tree of man,

she said, lowering her head in adoration. Inside the tree like a temple where incense swirled around an idol, O lord, lord, the pagan's pious love, the holy passion. I had wanted to cross over into Green Park and stroll through it, then cross into St. James's. But I cannot proceed. The bridge is a few feet away. But I cannot move one foot. I had wanted to keep going across London's green centre, then return the way I had gone, come again into Kensington Gardens. Instead, I turn back and find I can walk quite freely, adopting a marching rhythm, a military left-right, left-right, marching towards the Albert Memorial, there is nothing the matter with my legs, nothing has gone wrong though I know something has. Had he come this way, he would have gone striding on quickly over the bridge and goose-stepped past the tree with the hollow trunk, happy at the recollection of pleasure, the magical cave that he had entered with a woman as if taken by a priestess to an initiation. She was older. There was joy in her eyes when she beheld in him the boy-god and lowered her head in adoration, her tongue a sudden flame, and she no longer the priestess but the worshipper, lingam lover, red-hot like a glowing coal the tip of her tongue.

I stop and see if I cannot turn back. If I can walk so confidently in one direction then I should be able to do so in any other. And for a short distance I fling my arms, take on a jaunty air, and stride towards the bridge quite easily. But I stop and say there is no reason to go to the bridge. I've walked enough for one day. With that great hole in its trunk, that tree must have fallen by now. The woman in it, older than the boy she adored, her womb ached to succour a child. Enough for one day. I turn back. Her name was Grace, alas I had all but forgotten, the woman whose perfume he carried to his sleep. The woman now a spirit in the tree. Dead as the elms. Older, with that ache in her womb to breed, she worshipped him. In some park or heath at sunset, for she lived with her mother and he was a boy, and where else could they go but under elms and chestnuts and oaks in one of London's parks, two pagans watching the sun go down, twice weekly she made a shrine under the trees where she could worship him. Not true. Nothing religious about her ardour, nor his, and what's that piffle about two pagans, she a married woman too, abandoned and barely young, longing to fill an emptiness; and he a boy anxious for manhood, thrilled that she should take the lead, stroke him with her hand, and then raising her skirt, lying on the coat spread among ferns and bushes, part her legs and draw him in; he was amazed to see the bliss on her face and amazed too by his own luck, he had entered, and all because she had desired him and manipulated his lust, entered and so naturally fallen into a rocking rhythm that there seemed no other action in all of creation that could have any purpose. Dead as the elms, the old girl. None of that priestess and boy-god piffle either; nature, that's all. In London's parks, Hampstead and Blackheath and Putney and Richmond, in a circle of green around the city, and in its centre, returning again to Kensington, nature, that's all, the old bitch.

There's a scaffolding around the Albert Memorial and a green screen hung from the scaffolding. Prince Albert is being washed. He will be spick and span for the new century. He will emerge all bright and shiny from his bath. He will appear to be made of solid gold when he is unveiled; he will sit like an emperor of the universe, the single word ALBERT in gold at his feet. In one corner Europa riding her bull, in another, on an elephant, bejewelled Asia with solid breasts for England to suckle. I wonder if Albert and Victoria ever had a bath together—perfidious thought for one on Albion's soil—he sitting behind her in a tub filled with perfumed bubbles, her buttocks in his lap, his face leaning over the back of her head and bent above it as if he kissed the imperial crown, his hands through her arms soaping her breasts, working up a slippery lather, massaging the Empire's heart.

Maqsood Zaman was known as Max even when he was growing up in Bombay, so that when he went to school in England in the years not long after the end of the Second World War, a time when immigrants from the Commonwealth were rare and it was a trial for the English to have to pronounce a foreign name, it was convenient for him to say his name was Max.

Mr Watson, the double-chinned form master in the school in Chelsea, pushed back his black-rimmed spectacles while staring at the register and attempted to pronounce the foreign name. 'Mack-sued,' he stumbled over the two syllables, looked up, searching for the boy among the thirty in the class, stared down at the register again and continued, 'Za-za…Salmon! Macksued Salmon.'

The class laughed, and the inevitable class wit, Jimmy Langston who could never close his mouth on his yellowish crooked teeth, could think of nothing cleverer to say than, 'Thought there was a fishy smell in here', making his companions giggle.

'It's Max Simon, sir,' said Maqsood Zaman. He had prepared himself for this moment, having observed other Englishmen—the first of whom was the immigration officer at Tilbury—become perplexed when they looked at his name, as if it was something suspicious and contagious that had to be avoided.

'It's Max Simon, then,' the form master said, relieved that the strange combination of letters of the English alphabet was not a threat to his understanding. He lowered his head and put a mark in the register.

Jimmy Langston attempted another joke. 'It's Ganga Din from Madame Tussaud's Max Museum.' But the joke fell flat.

Mr Watson closed the register, gave Langston a stare, a look that silenced the other whisperers in the class for it signified an imminent cutting remark which might be amusing to hear, and pushing up his black-rimmed spectacles which had slipped down his nose before fixing his eyes on the dark boy, said, 'Well, Simon, you're new to our country, there are some forms of our language, *puns*, for instance—*which are sometimes silly*,' he said in a loud parenthesis, giving Langston another stare, 'and sometimes a cheap device with which to make people laugh—that might appear confusing to you.'

'Not at all, sir,' Max responded. 'I do not expect the complexities of the English language to constitute an impediment to my scholastic advancement.'

Several of the boys turned to look at Max. 'Wha' a mou'ful!' one muttered. Mr Watson removed his spectacles, went to clean them with a handkerchief which he drew from his right trouser pocket but seeing that the crumpled cloth was dirty and stained inserted it back into his pocket and put on his spectacles again. He gave Max a prolonged puzzled look, not sure whether to praise the foreign boy's vocabulary or criticize his verbosity, and instead, pointing a finger at another boy, said, 'Baker, could you be kind enough to give this class the benefit of your knowledge and define the word *impediment*?'

'Impediment,' Baker, who was not known for his scholarship, said, raising his eyes to the ceiling and thinking aloud, 'impediment, pediment, ped, ped is something to do with feet in Latin,' and, looking at the form master, said, 'putting one's foot into one's shoe, sir.'

The class laughed. 'What occasions the laughter?' Mr

Watson asked Merton, a short fat boy, who had laughed the loudest.

'Baker's put his foot into his mouth, sir,' Merton said, still laughing.

'I suppose you could give us a definition of *impediment*?' Mr Watson asked.

'Certainly, sir,' Merton answered. 'It's the triangular bit on the top of a building.'

This time only one boy, the pale and slim Robertson, laughed, so that the form master said, 'Well, Robertson?'

'Merton means pediment, sir, not *im*pediment,' Robertson said.

'Well, then,' Mr Watson said, 'enlighten us, Robertson.'

'Obstruction,' Robertson said. 'To be in the way, sir. The most famous use of the word is in the line, "Let me not to the marriage of true minds admit impediment".'

'Well, done, Robertson,' Mr Watson said, pleased that one of his best pupils had not let him down, and looking at Max, asked, 'Did you know that, Simon?'

'Robertson doesn't have it absolutely correct, sir,' Max answered. 'It is the opening of one of Shakespeare's sonnets. What Robertson quoted is not a line but a line and a half. Also, in the sonnet the word is not *impediment* but *impediments*, in the plural, sir, and it appears in the second line.'

Mr Watson pulled out his handkerchief, removed his spectacles, and looking with half-closed eyes at the class and without paying attention to the condition of his handkerchief proceeded to give the lenses a good rub. He put the handkerchief away, placed his spectacles back upon his nose, and opened his eyes wide. 'O bugger!' he muttered under his breath and to cover it up said aloud, 'O bother!' For he could see nothing but a cloudy smear. He removed his spectacles and realised the error of cleaning his glasses with a handkerchief into which he had earlier blown his nose. The boys had noticed, and while the form master tried to find a relatively clean corner of his handkerchief with which to make his spectacles serviceable, Merton said, 'There you have it, sir, one of the impediments of life.'

'You, Merton, need to be stuck into some pediment and left there to converse with a gargoyle,' Mr Watson countered, 'for all the understanding you have of your native tongue.'

'What's a gargoyle?' Merton quietly asked of a companion who answered, 'It's when a boy does it to a goyle and she goes, "Ga!".'

During recess Robertson found himself behind Baker in the queue at the tuck shop. As one of the fifth form's superior intellects, he had looked down upon Baker, but now said to him, 'Doesn't that bloke from India have a ghastly accent?' For his part, Baker cared little for the bookish types whose answers in class always made him appear stupid, but his tribal instinct told him that Robertson was drawing him into an alliance against the foreigner, and he answered, 'I'd say he has!'

The two walked out to the playground together, eating their buns. Baker was accustomed to being proven wrong in class but was now flattered that Robertson should have been so affronted by the foreign boy correcting his answer that he should want to team up with Baker to teach the darkie a lesson. What rankled with Robertson was that Max had given the appearance of being a superior scholar over a very trivial point; and when he thought about it, of course he knew, he said to himself, that the word was in the plural and that it was in the second line of the sonnet, for he had only been citing an example of the word *impediment*, not trying to prove anything to do with Shakespeare.

Two five-a-side games of soccer with a tennis ball and three separate games of cricket, also each with a tennis ball and lines chalked on the brick wall for stumps, all being played by the younger boys, were in progress in the crowded confusion of the playground; sometimes the two soccer games seemed to mingle into one which appeared to be played by two balls and frequently the three batsmen hit the ball across one another's pitch or into one of the soccer games; at the same time, many groups of three or four boys each strolled about the playground completely disregarding the territorial exclusivity which each of the games had theoretically marked out for itself; but the twenty or thirty players in the five games proceeded as if theirs was the only game, for habit had accustomed them to ignore the human chaos and, as if theirs was the exclusive engagement on the field, to eliminate from their consciousness any event or obstacle which was not part of their own game. Past the third of the cricket games, in the corner where the brick wall ended and the bicycle shed began, Merton stood with Max and a group of five or six boys to whom Merton was gleefully recounting Robertson's humiliation in the class. The short and fat Merton despised Robertson not because he constantly showed off his intellectual superiority in class but because he was tall and handsome, and coming out to the playground, Merton had sought out Max who stood alone by the bicycle shed and said to him, 'That was brilliant. Silly old Robertson thinks he's Rupert bloody Brooke.'

'What, he writes poems?' Max had asked. 'No,' answered Merton, 'only that he *looks* like Rupert Brooke.' Max remembered the picture of the poet who had died young, saw in his mind Robertson's resemblance to the portrait—a question of the line of the nose and the way the hair fell over the ear—and said, 'Oh, I see.' And then added, 'Never liked his poems.' Merton waved to some older boys and soon a group of them stood hearing him describe how Max had trumped Robertson. A mistimed shot from one of the cricket games sent the ball flying in the direction of the group where it would have hit the fair-haired sixth-former named Page but for Max putting his hand out and taking the catch. Page was the school's cricket captain and his eye caught the particular manner in which Max took the catch—to the ordinary eye nothing more than putting out a hand to catch a ball but to the cricketing expert there was in the gesture the skilled movement of an experienced player. 'Well caught,' he said, and added, 'do you bat or ball?' Max threw the ball to a fielder who had come running for it, and said, 'I open the batting and keep wicket.'

From the middle of the crowd where he strolled with Baker, Robertson saw Page talking to Max and even from a distance he could read the expression on Page's face as friendly to the foreigner. He did not want Baker to see that Max might have the cricket captain as his friend and steered him in the opposite direction, saying, 'There's Langston, let's get him to join us.' Langston grinned when he saw them approaching. Crumbs from the bun he was eating were stuck among his crooked teeth. 'Feeling *imp*ish, are you,' he said, 'or just on a *ped*estrian lark,' and, kicking the ground, added, 'on this hard ce*ment*.'

'You're a born wit,' Robertson flattered him. 'What do you say, we put up an impediment for this foreign upstart?'

'Salmon, as old Watson first called him,' Langston said, 'has to be taught that swimming against the current is awfully dangerous for his health.'

'Precisely,' Robertson said. 'Will you not therefore go fishing with your good friend Fraser?'

'Oh, Fraser will like that,' Langston said. Fraser was the

school captain, and Langston, only recently appointed a prefect, his most sycophantic supporter. 'Fraser will fry him in hot oil,' he added.

The following Monday morning, Max was walking to the school when just as he was passing, a hundred yards from the school entrance, the newsagent's where the boys bought their sweets, he was stopped by Baker who at that moment came out of the shop and almost bumped into him. 'Oh, sorry!' Baker said, and then quickly added, 'I say, weren't you half clever in the answer you gave Mr Gorman?'

The reference was to a class the previous Thursday when the Latin master had asked a question that not only Max had been the only boy in the class able to answer but, giving the answer, he had also embellished it with a lengthy quotation, recited from memory, from Horace. Max was pleased by Baker's praise and allowed himself the luxury of hearing a longer critical acclaim of two other instances when he had excelled intellectually. When they were about to walk on to the school, Baker pointed to the cards pinned in a small display window by the entrance to the newsagent's and said, 'You ever read these? You're clever with words, see what you make of this one here.' Max leaned his head forward and spoke aloud the two words in capital letters above a phone number, BOTTOMS CANED, and then looked at Baker and said, 'Must be someone who works with wicker, caning chairs.' Baker laughed. 'It's not the

bottoms of chairs,' he said, 'it's the bottoms of old gee-
zers who get their pleasure being flogged.' He read aloud
the words on another card—ORGAN TUNING—
and challenged Max to interpret them. Max realised
that many of the cards apparently offering some rou-
tine housekeeping service were cryptic solicitations for
custom from prostitutes. Amused by the word play, he
became absorbed in reading and interpreting some more.
Baker suddenly said, 'Gosh, we're going to be late!' The
two hastily walked away and made for the school. The
bell had already rung, the playground was empty. When
he had set out from home, Max had timed himself to
arrive just before the bell, but held up by Baker's flattery
and then by reading the cards, he now saw that they were
both late. 'Bugger it,' he heard Baker say, 'it's flippin'
Fraser on duty.'

They were five minutes late. The school captain
himself stood at the gate, a little notebook in his hand.
The two were stopped. Fraser looked at Max severely.
'Name?' he asked.

'Max Simon.'

Fraser stared at him icily. 'As it is in the class register,'
he said.

'Maqsood Zaman.'

Fraser lowered his notebook and slightly turned
his body so that Max could see what he was writing.
'MUCKSOOT SOMEONE,' he wrote.

'It's M-A-Q . . .' Max began to spell the name out

correctly, but Fraser cut him off, saying, 'I do not need your assistance with English spelling, thank you.' He gave Max another icy stare and then pronounced his sentence: 'An hour's detention for being late and a second hour tomorrow for giving a false name when first asked.'

'But everyone knows me as Max Simon!' Max protested, 'Even Mr Watson calls me that.'

Fraser looked at him with contempt and said, 'You don't become English by making your name sound English. And you do not argue with the school captain.'

'It's not fair,' Max said and began to go towards the school door.

'Just a minute,' came the cold, harsh voice and he turned back to see Fraser glaring angrily at him. 'I did not say you could go,' Fraser said. 'That will be an hour the day after tomorrow for disobedience.' He made a mark in his notebook. Max involuntarily stamped his foot and again said, though in a restrained voice, 'It's not fair'. Fraser gave him another angry stare. 'That is insubordination,' he said coldly and made another mark in his notebook. 'You are given an hour's detention after school each day this week.' He paused and again stared at Max before saying coldly. 'Now, go to class.'

Max stood there for a moment, staring back angrily at Fraser. Fraser looked at Baker and said, 'I'm surprised at you, Baker. You haven't been late before and now you're learning foreign habits. I'm going to let you off with a warning this time.'

Max walked away while Fraser continued to speak to Baker. He looked back when he entered the school building and saw Fraser laugh at something Baker had just said and the two boys, both laughing now, begin to walk together towards the entrance to the school building.

During the morning break, Max saw from a distance a group of boys earnestly listening to what Baker was telling them. Robertson, standing opposite Baker with Langston next to him, noticed Max across the playground, and catching Langston's attention, flicked his head in the direction of Max. The two boys smiled knowingly.

Victoria Regina. Empress of India. Bathed in Albert's love. Mourned his early death by placing the four corners of the world below his feet and in his golden splendour garbing her prince in the robes of a Roman imperator rex. High on his pedestal, behind the green screen hung from the scaffolding, Albert is being restored to life. The black soot of post-war London is being scrubbed away, the decline and fall of empire substituted by nostalgia for an age of gold and glory. Rule, Britannia. *Clippety-clop, tippety-tip*. Strange to hear horses' hooves. But there they are. A string of ponies on Kensington Road, young girls in fleece-lined leather jackets and black riding hats ambling past the Albert Hall. I watch them proceed towards Alexandra Gate, taking their time, unmindful of the queue of buses obliged to crawl behind them. Some pedestrians on the pavement stop and watch them go. A man with a camera takes a picture, trots after them and takes another picture, bending down to a squatting position to do so, and then stands up, holds the camera against his chest, looks at the young girls and smiles, pleased that he has recorded a scene that doesn't come every tourist's way and which he'll show all his friends, *Look, how English this is*, he will say, *in the middle of London, can you imagine, how very English*. More buses and cars are held up all the way to Palace Gate. No one minds being held up. *So English*, says another tourist on the pavement. The girls ride their ponies at a gentle and unhurried pace, complacently confident in their aristocratic presumption that the world waits upon them. The people in the buses, when they see what has held them up, do not look annoyed but pleased rather, as if they had contributed to the preservation of some ancient privilege, that the girls were owed this indulgence, a nice democratic courtesy extended to the nobility. The girls turn into the park and make for Rotten Row. Across the road, a 73 bus has stopped outside the Albert Hall. A group of people alights and walks hastily to the box office. A concert perhaps. Not the season for the Proms though. The three summers he lived there, he walked from Drayton Gardens to the Albert Hall. Stood there with the buoyant promenaders. Purcell, Elgar, Holst. The promenaders cheered Sir Malcolm heartily. Music to swell the heart. Pomp and Circumstance. He cheered with the crowd which bobbed on waves of patriotism. *Bravo!* A man standing near him looked at him, a puzzled expression on his face, unsure if his own patriotic zeal was not being mocked by the stranger in the English midst. Rule, Britannia. How absurd another people's patriotism. I retrace my steps past Albert Memorial towards the Flower Walk. Cars coming up from Exhibition Road are making for the Serpentine bridge. Sunlight flashes from their windows. Past them, between the swift, momentary gaps which appear between one bumper and the next in the succession of cars and taxis, I see the girls on the ponies trotting away on Rotten Row, their black-helmeted heads rising and falling as if they were nodding in eager acquiescence to some proposal. I wonder if one of the girls is named Imogen. A favourite name of that class. Virginal heroines of the Romances. Marina, Miranda, Imogen. But not Perdita. Never heard of a girl named Perdita. Parents would be daft to name a daughter Perdita. Would be asking for bad luck. The lost one. Best to name her Imogen. Full-cheeked white round face, blue eyes, always a smile on her lips, her breasts so small at fifteen she looks almost like a boy, so innocent and beautiful, Imogen. *A pudency so rosy* . . . A word to dream on, pudency . . . *that I thought her chaste as unsunned snow.* But she *was* a boy, the Imogen who's sprung in my mind! The pale round-faced fourth former Bosanquet the headmaster cast as Imogen in his all-boy production. An annual event at the school, the headmaster's Shakespeare. As-he-was-performed-in-his-own-day. Boys as girls. Explains why he never put on *Macbeth*. No boy could play Lady MacBitch. Genetically impossible. There was a schoolboy production at Stonyhurst where they got around the problem by eliminating Lady Macbeth and replacing her with Uncle Donald. God knows what Uncle Donald did with *unsex me here* and the *babe that milks me*. Someone must have played her in the bard's time, though. Bosanquet was so pretty dressed up as Imogen one of the sixth formers suddenly kissed him on the mouth in a break during the dress rehearsal and messed up his lipstick. I have come out at the end of the Flower Walk, just across from Palace Gate where I had entered an hour ago, and realise that I have, these last ten minutes, walked the whole length of the Flower Walk without seeing a single thing. All phenomena vanished from the planet. Not a particle of dust in the air. I must have seen the weeping birch, the pansies, the palm trees and envisioned again the palm trees in the tropics, in an oasis, west, I can fix the place now, of the Andes, in the narrow burning plain before the land falls into the Pacific. Could even have stopped and had a childish dialogue with the squirrel, pretending to offer it a nut, and the little creature, seeing nothing in my hand, might have spat out an angry clicking from its throat and scampered away. I must have remembered seeing, and therefore seen him in my mind which would instantly have

invented more fictions of his future history, the little boy
Jeremy waving like a miniature astronaut, and aware of
his presence in my imagination must have looked round
to see if he was not still there with his mother following
him, the camera ready in her hand for a candid shot.
But I did not see anything. As if I was not in the Flower
Walk at all. A pudency so rosy. The headmaster was
annoyed and wanted to know why Imogen's makeup
was smudged. 'I was hungry, sir,' Bosanquet explained,
'and ate a bun rather quickly.' The headmaster looked
aghast. 'A *bun?* Ate *quickly?*' His cry echoed in the hall,
and echoes still under the pale sky as I step across the
Broad Walk, and remember just then remembering earlier when I had come out of the Flower Walk—what,
forty, fifty minutes ago?—the phrase I had not quoted
to Stannie from Woolf's Diary, *& time shall be utterly
obliterated*, when we sat with our half-pints in the Goat,
and remembering the unspoken phrase just when the
echo of the headmaster's voice died under the pale sky,
heard then the diarist's voice as if she spoke in my ear
while she wrote her next line, *My theory being that the
actual event practically does not exist—nor time either.*

A 49 bus is standing at the top of Palace Gate, waiting for the light to change before turning towards the
High Street. A double-decker with its conductor standing next to the cavity for luggage on the platform at the
rear, the familiar old London Transport double-decker
that will be replaced on your next visit by the nimble

single-decked Armchair buses and then again by the
new double-deckers. You always sat in the upper deck
and smoked two cigarettes between Clapham Junction
and where you got off just past Barker's in High Street,
Ken. Sometimes, because the traffic in the High Street
was barely moving and the smoke and the diesel fumes
were making you nauseous, you got off the bus, besides
you could walk faster to Brenda's flat off Church Street.
Past De Vere Gardens, then across the road zig-zagging
through the stationary traffic, past Kensington Palace
Gardens where a Rolls-Royce waited to join the traffic
and blocked the pedestrians on the pavement, the chauf-
feur sitting with dove-grey gloved hands on the steering wheel, a disdainful expression frozen on his face. A
lady seen through the window behind him, ghostly pale
in the Silver Shadow, a fur stole upon her shoulders,
the neck exposed though, a flash of sapphire there, a
glint of diamonds at the pale, veiny neck. She raised
a hand to look at the time when you stood there on
the pavement, your passage blocked, a bony hand with
long fingers, sparkle of diamonds surrounding a sapphire ring, gold at the wrist, time trapped in a tiny circle of diamonds on a gold bracelet, the bare forearm
thin and veiny. *A bracelet of bright hair about the bone.*
You walked round the front of the car to go past it.
Sometimes, after alighting prematurely from the 49 bus,
you did not cross the road till you had reached Barker's
and had dawdled there a quarter of an hour staring at

the clothes in the windows; and becoming possessed by
the hypothesis of affluence, you saw what you could be
and were so in thrall to the projections of vanity that
sometimes you walked on, acquiring conjectural posses-
sions from the succeeding windows, and proceeded past
other stores, past Ponting's, past Derry and Tom's, past
Dolcis, past Meeker's until you had furnished a house
in Kensington Square and filled your wardrobe with silk
shirts, suits of West Country wool, cashmere sweaters,
Bally shoes, walking in your moneyed dream past Adam
and Eve Mews; then, snapping out of the hypnosis of
future opulence, you crossed the High Street to go to
Brenda's flat and walked hastily back until you reached
St Mary Abbots Church, just past the library where
you saw him among the shelves picking out Dowden's
Shelley. His heart would not burn. The Parish Church
of Kensington. *Open minds. Open hearts. Open for
prayer*—you will read on a future visit on its large blue
sign fixed to the iron railing blocking off a glimpse of
patchy grass. Around the corner and up Church Street,
then. Sometimes, the 49 bus you had abandoned had
still not reached Barker's. That sapphire necklace would
look marvellous on Brenda, the gold bracelet too with
the watch in its circle of diamonds. The tiny little hands
doing their 24-hour rounds, the minute hand pointing
to a diamond every quarter of an hour, valuable and pre-
cious, time. Marvellous on Brenda with her dreamy eyes
which, when she looked at you under the rare pressure

of a sudden emotion surging unexpectedly within her breast, sparkled. The bus has at last joined the traffic to the High Street.

No sign of him in the crowd concentrated beside the zebra crossing. Perhaps he had not been on his way to Kensington Gardens but had been coming up Gloucester Road to go to Maurice's flat in Emperor's Gate and being early had loitered up to kill time browsing in Karnac Books and then succumbed to the temptation of revisiting the fantasy of his future house in Launceston Place, waiting till it was five minutes after he was expected at Maurice's before looping back to Emperor's Gate.

No gate to an emperor's palace, no blue plaque to commemorate a poet's brief bedsitting residence there, greater though the poet proved to be than the two Edwards and the two Georges who succeeded globular Victoria, bejewelled emperors all of India, only a cul-de-sac dormitory, Emperor's Gate, for solicitors' clerks and novice stockbrokers and advertising copy writers, new dreamers of imperial wealth, who could walk round the corner to Gloucester Road and take the tube to Holborn and Temple and Bank, a good address, Emperor's Gate, where Maurice lived, who had said to Max, 'Come Friday evening'.

A light blue linen suit, the single-breasted jacket unbuttoned, a pale-yellow tie loosely knotted, Maurice affected a dashing informality and though proportioned as an athlete he gasped for breath like one twice his weight and complained of the heat though the summer remained unrelievedly cool and wet. Parted at the side above his left ear and neatly combed straight across his head, his blond hair, as well as his eyebrows of a lighter shade above sharply blue eyes, gave him a golden-boyish look while his thin-lipped mouth, often open to draw breath, made him appear somewhat perplexed, so that while his expressive eyes were those of one who at an exhibition of new paintings cannot repress his delighted admiration for what he sees, the mouth confessed to being puzzled by what the art represented.

A recital at the French Lycée at South Ken. A Frenchman at the piano, another standing next to it, singing, *Zanzibar! Vous êtes en Paris.* An enraptured audience listening to modern French music as it might have been performed in a salon in Paris. Nearly moist-eyed, sunk in nostalgia, the French in the audience, as if in some distant foreign land, Martinique or Guyana, dreaming of far-away France. Max there in the fourth row with six other boys and Mr Harrison, the young Englishman with the French haircut who wore a red bowtie, newly arrived at the school to assist Mr Little, the old teacher of French, and who in his youthful enthusiasm had formed a club of seven sixth-formers, giving them Rimbaud and Mallarmé to read and took them to see an Alain Resnais film at the Academy in Oxford Street and to hear Poulenc and Satie at the

Lycée, obsessively planning excursions into French culture, for Mr Harrison the world outside France was the
realm of the barbarians. His enthusiasm for French culture had been fervently adopted by the group of sixth-
formers, persuading them they belonged to an exclusive
society with its secret rituals and pilgrimages to exotic
sites. Max had taken to wearing a bowtie, a green one
with red dots. *Oui, Monsieur Arisonne!* he and the boys
were heard to say frequently. The man at the piano gently raised himself a few inches from the stool and then
firmly lowered himself on the cushion while simultaneously striking the keys and the man standing next to
him repeated for the fourth time the refrain, *Zanzibar!*
Vous êtes en Paris. Max turned his head to his right and
the corner of his eye received the impression that someone was staring at him. He quickly looked ahead and
saw the pianist's shoulders swaying slightly and then
turned his head again to the right, this time sharply. At
the end of the fifth row a man in a light-blue suit and
pale-yellow tie seemed to have been studying his profile and now, being momentarily held by Max's eyes,
smiled weakly and turned away his gaze. During the
interval Mr Harrison took the boys aside to a corner of
the hall and had just begun to talk about his favourite
composer when he spotted the man in the light blue suit
standing across the hall, visible only in glimpses because
people were passing in front of him to go out the door
beside which he stood, aborted his talk in mid-sentence

and said, 'Talk of Ravel, here's another Maurice, my old friend Fallowes!' They had been at Oxford together, he quickly explained to the boys before excusing himself to go to his friend whom he had not seen since the two had come down three years ago. Max observed the two men clasp hands warmly and not let go for a full minute or longer after a vigorous shake. Though their words could not be distinguished, the sound of their voices, deeply resonant of the festive camaraderie of bosom compan-ions, carried across the hall, mixed with little bursts of laughter that attested to the gaiety of their shared past. Those of the audience who had wanted to go out had all done so by now, some still remained in their seats conversing in low voices, though with an occasional loud emphasis, the French phrases now soft, distant and melodious and now suddenly sounding as if a fist had hit the piano. While his fellow schoolboys talked—as usual the tall black-haired Morillon, who claimed Norman descent and therefore believed that he not only had the most to say about matters concerning France but also that whatever he said was the incontestable truth, had launched on a monologue—Max glanced across the hall at Mr Harrison and his friend Maurice Fallowes who now stood with their backs to the wall, so that while they continued their conversation their eyes were not upon each other but looked across the room at Max. Mr Harrison seemed to be doing most of the talking, as if answering some question his friend had asked. Two or three times, Mr Harrison turned his head and looked at his companion, giving his head a little jerk, as when one makes a significant point. His companion, however, kept his eyes fixed upon Max. In the meanwhile, among the boys, Morillon, a fringe of black hair falling across his pale white forehead, continued his soliloquy, and hearing him say, '. . . so much for d'Indy, but of course, for sheer purity of musical ideas nothing compares with Reynaldo Hahn's *L'Ile du Rêve*, which for sheer compositional . . .', Max suspected Morillon of imitating those priests who made a great impression upon an ignorant congregation by repeating as their own theological ideas of dubious worth which, moreover, they had not understood but had cynically adopted because their portentous phraseology and obscure references sounded intellectually intimidating. Morillon's speech became an incoherent murmur in his consciousness as, responding to a beckoning gesture from Mr Harrison, Max began to walk between two rows of empty chairs to where his teacher stood with his friend. 'Simon,' Mr Harrison said when Max was still a few paces away, 'you're from India, you can settle this dispute. Oh . . .' he interrupted himself, for Max had reached the two men, 'Maurice, this is my bright sixth-former Max Simon, Simon meet my old friend from Oxford, Maurice.' Max held up his hand, surprised that Mr Harrison had only given his friend's Christian name, and just as Maurice clasped the proffered hand, Max heard the teacher continue,

'Maurice here thinks the Gateway of India is in Delhi, not Bombay.' His handshake with Maurice completed, Max made to withdraw his hand but felt it being clasped firmly. He saw Maurice staring at him, smiling, as if he wished the boy would prove him right. 'They are two different monuments,' Max said, 'The Gateway of India is in Bombay, the one in Delhi is called India Gate.' Maurice quickly raised his left hand and pressed it against the back of Max's hand which Maurice still clasped firmly with his right, and said, 'How terribly clever of you!' Max was about to respond that the question was too trivial to represent his correct answer as a measure of his cleverness but he was flattered by the Englishman's attention and simply said, 'It's nothing.' The interval was about to end, people had begun to return to their chairs. Maurice at last let go of Max's hand, withdrawing his own two hands slowly, the fingertips sliding softly across the palm and the back of Max's hand and pausing for a second at the fingertips before falling away. There was so much he still needed to learn about India, he said quickly, if only there were time, he really was terribly ignorant, an absolute imbecile, 'No use pretending I'm not!', didn't Harrison think Max would be a perfect teacher, now there's an idea, well, why not, come Friday evening, 'Come on any Friday,' the flat's in Emperor's Gate, not far from where they were, just off Gloucester Road. 'Oh, I know,' Max said, 'I go past there almost every day.' Which indeed he did, living then in Drayton Gardens, and only later in Clapham when, travelling in the 49 bus, he again found himself regularly going up Gloucester Road, never failing to see his schoolboy self, seventeen-year-old Max, sporting his green, red-dotted bowtie, walking into Emperor's Gate for his first visit to Maurice, wondering what questions he would ask about India.

All very imperial, the Gloucester Road neighbour-hood, Queen's Gate, Palace Gate, Emperor's Gate, Max remarked and fancied the image of London as a large cauldron in which melted the heaped gold from India. He paused to glance at a notice outside St Stephen's Church Hall—ugly yellow brick, ugly white-painted triple-arched entrance, so ugly so much of modern eccle-siastical architecture—looked at his watch to make sure he was no more than five minutes late and turned into the triangular cul-de-sac with its little triangular garden in the middle. Restful to the eyes after St Stephen's the chestnut tree, the two plane trees, the bushes, and two other trees, beeches, he was not sure, but let his eyes be filled with their green before walking on to keep his appointment with Maurice.

Maurice shared the flat with a young solicitor and Max's first visit coincided with a party the latter had thrown to celebrate his engagement to a dark-haired woman whose greater height, by some three inches, and width, or that charming female plumpness that makes the skirt spread out rather grandly at the waist, gave her

the appearance of being eagerly possessive and assert-
ively dominant when she danced with her pliant fiancé.
There was a crowd of young couples dancing in the con-
fined space of the drawing room where the carpet had
been rolled up. Max heard Alma Cogan's voice from the
gramophone when he came up the steps and found the
door to the flat open. He saw Maurice dancing with
a tall dark-haired older woman and Maurice, noticing
him, smiled and made a welcoming gesture by jerking
his head and continued to dance. Max stood in a corner
by a hat stand from which hung five or six umbrellas
and one bowler hat. Not as yet knowing the occasion
for the party and feeling himself an intruder, he wondered whether he had not chosen the wrong day for his
visit. But Maurice had said, 'Come on any Friday', and
this was the third Friday after the recital at the Lycée.
Perhaps Maurice and his flat mate threw a party every
Friday. Max knew nothing about this world. It was the
first time he had come to a party where people drank and
danced. They did more. He saw a dark-haired lady seemingly gather up her young man, clasp his head tightly a
moment within her bosomy amplitude, hold it suddenly
in both her hands and attack his lips with her open
mouth. Other couples danced around them. Max was
both aroused and repelled. He thought that perhaps he
should go away. There were eight or nine other young
women, each with her partner, two not dancing so
much as merely gliding slowly about the floor while held

tightly in their partner's embrace. Most of the women were attractive, two quite thrillingly beautiful, but held in the arms of men with whom they exchanged signals of mutual desire, and therefore they were unlikely even to acknowledge Max's presence in the room. They were engaged in their native rituals, and he, though in his second year in London, was still fresh out of India and to his perception English behaviour contained anthropological surprises and oddities. He decided to leave. Maurice, watching him over the shoulder of his partner, said something to her, left her and walked to Max who was just then making to go. 'Sorry not to have greeted you when you came but as you saw I was in the clutches of dear old Deirdre.' But Max mustn't wait another minute before getting himself a drink. He would join him. It was hot work, dancing. The drinks were in the other room. 'Come,' he added, taking Max's hand and leading him past the dancing couples and the abandoned Deirdre who was walking towards a bedroom. Ah yes, sherry, Maurice exclaimed, just the thing in this weather, a glass of pale sherry, didn't Max think it the best drink, sitting sunk in a sofa, sipping sherry, away from the clutches of women like Deirdre, enjoying the conversation of a man, wasn't that the most civilised thing in the world, a conversation about poetry, Max must quote him some, Harrison had told him he was a poet, he should not be repeating to Max what Harrison had told him, 'But this is only between the two of us,' he said conspiratorially, coming close to Max's ear and almost brushing it with his lips, a confidence between two good friends, surely there was nothing wrong with that, yes, Harrison had remarked Max was quite exceptionally talented, a new Keats, Harrison had said, ah, here you are, the sherry! Max, who had never drunk sherry, felt elated: this was the moment, he was certain he would look back on it, when he had achieved adulthood. 'I'm more Shelley than Keats,' he said, holding the glass and watching Maurice pour himself one, and added without thinking, 'A Shelley devoted to sherry.' Maurice laughed and said, 'That's good, Shelley and sherry, terribly good, you're a born wit!' Max himself harboured no such delusion about the quality of his wit but allowed himself to be flattered, experiencing an exquisite pleasure that the praise for his speech came from an Englishman. He took his first sip of sherry and just before the initial drop of the golden liquid rolled towards his tongue he anticipated a deliciousness that exceeded anything he had ever experienced from a drink. Nothing happened, his tongue felt no novel sensation. He tilted the glass, took a more generous sip. Far from delicious; indeed, medicinal. But not wanting to appear unsophisticated and thinking there must be something special as yet unrevealed to him if the drink was so favoured by the English, he held the glass in front of his nose and said, 'Thou breath of Autumn's being,' and smiling, turned his head to look at Maurice, who, smiling too, said, 'You *are* a beautiful poet!', a remark which, though pleasingly flattering, suggested to Max that Maurice had not realised that the phrase was not Max's but Shelley's. Perhaps it was only a moment's forgetfulness. Max could not believe that an Englishman could be so ignorant of his own culture. Perhaps Maurice was only pretending to be ignorant out of kindness to a foreigner who could not know that what he took to be beauty in the Englishman's language was to the native a common phrase that repeated usage had converted to a cliché; and to test this supposition, he seized the opportunity a moment later, when Maurice remarked how the weather still continued cold, to quote, 'If Winter comes, can Spring be far behind?', and was at first confused by Maurice spontaneously squeezing his shoulder and leaning forward to plant a sudden kiss on his cheek and then shocked on hearing him say, as he leaned back again, 'You're such a natural poet, old Harrison was right', for Max's first impression had been correct, Maurice was ignorant, a notion that was confirmed when he added, 'You really must bring me some of your poems', though once again Max sought a reason to excuse him and thought it must be the famous English diffidence, not wishing to threaten another's self-esteem with a show of one's cleverness, besides Max was becoming increasingly charmed by the Englishman's interest in him. It had not been much more than five years, Britain still then the imperial power, when an Indian could not even approach an Englishman let alone have any friendly relationship with him—and as for English women, they resided in some galaxy so remote that an Indian even with an astronomer's vision could not have located them in his universe. Mystery and magic surrounded the sons and daughters of England, and on the rare occasion that an Englishman had any business with an Indian the latter became a figure of awe, admiration and envy among his fellow countrymen. Maurice's hand still on his shoulder, images flowed through Max's mind of seeing English soldiers in Bombay, but always from a distance, and perspiring pink-faced Englishmen in white jacket and tie arriving with their bejewelled and gorgeously gowned wives in a Morris or a Humber, and sometimes a Rolls Royce, for a dance at the Taj hotel, always so immaculate and aloof the English in India, and here he was, an Englishman's hand on his shoulder, the warm, moist touch of the Englishman's lips still creating a sensation on his cheek so strange he could not tell whether what had pressed against his flesh had been a lump of ice or a red-hot coal.

A pause in the music in the drawing room had brought some people in search of refreshment and four of them were standing beside the drinks table at the moment when Maurice leaned forward and kissed Max's cheek. Max noticed that while the group at the table seemed to pay no attention to the two of them in the sofa, a young woman, whom he saw looking at him a second before Maurice's lips touched his cheek, reached up towards her male companion's ear and said something, prompting the man to look first at Max and then at Maurice, his eyes narrowing a moment and then opening wide in the expression of one who suddenly understands a situation, whereupon he turned to the woman and lowering himself whispered something in her ear and she, nodding her head slightly, glanced quickly at Max with bright, knowing eyes, and the two walked away, drinks in hand. Max wondered whether their glances and whispering implied a reprimand or at least a mild disapproval that Maurice should appear intimate with an Indian and in a spontaneous gesture of defiance against lingering imperial hauteur he put his hand upon Maurice's on his shoulder and pressed it gently. Maurice smiled, his eyes brightening.

Max took another sip of his sherry and felt a pleasant warm sensation in his throat. The taste on his tongue was no longer medicinal. He was surprised to see that he had already drunk almost all there was in his glass. When could he have done it, they hadn't been there more than ten minutes, perhaps a bit longer, he hadn't looked at the time, but funny how familiar the taste had become, as if he'd been drinking sherry all his life, yes, he would have another glass, he accepted, when Maurice offered to refill it. The music began again. People came for drinks and went back to the dancing. One couple came in, placed their empty glasses on the table, turned and clasped each other tightly, joined their lips for a long kiss, opened their mouths for a mutual penetration of tongues, suddenly held back their faces and looked at each other in astonishment and wonder and as suddenly reunited their mouths for a minute longer, stopped, refilled their glasses and walked away. While they had stood, another young woman had come in, looked around distractedly, paying no attention to the kissing couple, poured herself half a glass of sherry and returned to the drawing room, throwing a vague, almost unseeing, glance at Max's right thigh where Maurice's hand had just landed. Max saw the hand begin to stroke the thigh gently and the fingers make tentative probes towards the buttons on the trouser fly, producing a curiously satisfying sensation which yet he thought he ought to inhibit, and transferring the sherry glass to his left hand he went to push away Maurice's hand with his but just then a burst of applause and cries of approbation mixed with laughter distracted them and they rose quickly and walked towards the door to the drawing room. A young woman in a wide-collared pale green V-necked satin blouse with mother-of-pearl buttons and a bright orange flaring skirt that fell to below her knees was taking a bow, her head bent low so that her fine blond hair hung loose in wild disarray; she raised her head, stood erect, turning her head right and left, smiling at her admirers, for several people were still clapping softly, held her skirt at either hip, drawing it up a little, and made little curtsies, looking shyly at the men, smiling. No doubt it was her remarkable beauty that had elicited the applause. There was a silken luxury to her fine blond hair, parted at the side, a little above her right ear, which framed her face; her large dark eyes were touchingly frank, suggesting a sublimely innocent character, as she gazed with a trusting openness at the men regarding her with predatory stares, each one eager to snatch her virtue, a common male condition from which Max was not exempt. Though there was a touch of gaudiness about her painted lips and the rouge at her cheeks, the excesses in her make-up heightened her innocent aspect, giving her the appearance of being sexually naïve, one whose essays at highlighting her beauty were still crudely experimental. But in those facets of a female figure that hold the greatest fascination for a man, drawing his covetous eye from the breast's rounded abundance to the hip's curvature, nature had blessed her so benignly that she needed no artificial assistance to guarantee that wherever she appeared no male eye would want to turn away its fevered gaze from her body. Then she spoke—a shrugging of the shoulders, the raising of the hands and turning the palms upwards in a questioning gesture—and asked, 'Why has the music stopped?'

The blood within Max that had become so agitated while he stood in the doorway entranced by female beauty that he could hear it throbbing at his temples, took a sudden leap. The voice was a man's. As soon as this knowledge came to him, the face that had appeared so beautiful was transformed to a grotesque mask, every feature that was associated with desire now elicited revulsion, and where, as long as the female illusion lasted, he would never have known who it was he was looking at, now that his imagination had with a sudden involuntary convulsion peeled away the make-up, he immediately recognised the man: Mr Harrison.

Max excused himself and left Maurice, giving him the impression that he was going in search of a toilet. Mr Harrison, in the middle of a crowd of admirers, had not seen Max. Trying to remain unnoticed by Mr Harrison, Max stealthily made his way around the room until he gained the obscurity of the small entrance hall and quietly let himself out of the flat. In the future, when Mr Harrison appeared in the classroom in his red bowtie or took the boys to some function at the Lycée, Max would never let him know that he had seen him in the guise of a woman.

Then why did he return to Emperor's Gate? Mr Harrison had not been the only transvestite there, he understood in retrospect. The illusion of female sexuality had been the most potent where painted beauty had been the most thrilling to behold, and he felt his tumescent male response rudely mocked by his retrospective understanding that there had been no female organ at the very spot on the person's anatomy that had aroused his keenest desire. He could have no doubt as to Maurice's intentions. Why then did he return to Emperor's Gate? Maurice was alone in the flat the following Friday. There was a moment's look of incomprehension on his face, as if he did not know the youth with the green bowtie, then he smiled and pulled back the door, opening it wide to welcome him in. Was it to affirm to himself whether Maurice would continue what he had begun and, if he resumed, towards what end would he proceed, why had he returned to Emperor's Gate?

No sign of him now. The crowd at the zebra crossing at the top of Palace Gate thins and swells, first there is just one man with a golden retriever and when you look a moment later there are twenty or thirty men and women there, but when everyone has gone, crossed over and entered Kensington Gardens or is walking on the pavement along the railing towards the High Street, the view down Palace Gate is unobstructed. Clearly no sign of him. Off in that 49 bus to go to Church Street, to Brenda's. Gone past Emperor's Gate a long while ago, witnessing again the youth in the green bowtie with red dots walking up Emperor's Gate that other time, no sign of him now. Most unusual this weather, this light with such depth. More sleepy than dreamy, Brenda's eyes, a laziness rather, an ocular reluctance, but brightly awakened by a sudden emotional charge in rare moments when she could no longer remain unresponsive to his embrace.

Not very satisfactory, that way of putting it. The alternatives that appear in one's perception are constantly reinvesting the past with an existential vigour or perhaps are suggestive merely of a common sentimentality which is flatteringly observed as a source of unique suffering. Two separate times, two separate points of attraction pulling him this way and that, but while with Brenda he knew what he wanted, and did not obtain it, with Maurice he was curious as to what was wanted of him though he knew in advance that he would refuse whatever was asked, which implied that he had a firm idea of what was about to be asked just as he was fixed in his own idea of what he wanted from Brenda. Recovering from his initial surprise and confusion when he'd opened the door and seen Max, Maurice said he'd been hoping desperately to see him again. Come, he added suddenly holding his hand and leading him to the room where they'd sat together the previous time, let's have some sherry. Where was Danny, the young solicitor who shared the flat with him, Oh, he answered, he's having one of those jolly festive evenings with his future in-laws that in reality are an embarrassing bore, it's what people have to suffer when they insist on doing their duty. But, he said and stopped, handing Max a glass, his eyes roaming across the features of Max's face and then fixing upon his lips. But. Max waited. Half a minute perhaps; whereupon Maurice turned around to pour himself a glass and with his back to Max said he was going away to west Africa the following week, to Accra, the company he worked for, Lever Brothers, were sending him to Ghana for six months. 'Do you know,' he said, one hand raising a glass to his lips and the other pointing to the sofa, 'I'm an expert'—the two just then sitting down next to each other—'on coconuts?' Max said he loved coconuts, after all, he'd grown up on the Malabar coast, but was surprised to hear Maurice say, 'That's another thing we have in common.' Not surprised, however, that Maurice patted his thigh as he spoke and kept his hand there as he proceeded to sip from his glass, his glance fixed upon Max's eyes; and as if to test the boy's inclination he squeezed his thigh and moved his fingers like one tuning a guitar. After the first year at the school where his position as a dark foreigner with a funny name had kept him without friends, Max had begun to be accepted by the boys because of his brilliance as a cricketer and admired by the teachers for the poems he published in the school magazine. He had formed two special friendships, one with a fellow batsman and another with a boy who shared his enthusiasm for modern poetry; and among the teachers there was Mr Harrison who had included him in his little elite group of sixth-formers and also the dashing assistant master of English, Charles Bitterman, who, noticing that the somewhat old-fashioned rather flowery prose of his essays yet had a curious freshness, gave him modern writers like Orwell to read and, seeing the speed with which Max improved his prose style, began to take a close personal interest in his writing. His was the natural human impulse to be so integrated in a social group that one's individual characteristics are

indistinguishable from those of the majority while at
the same time to be appreciated for some special talent
that one's individuality is conspicuously highlighted.
Growing up in Bombay when the British ruled India,
Max had observed that the English made no connections with the natives; they remained segregated, remote,
and fostered an aura of themselves as a superior race.
And coming to England at first gave him the feeling
an untouchable might experience among Brahmins in
a shrine they had reserved exclusively for themselves.
Acceptance by the group was a slow and a humiliating
procedure, so that the sweetness of his success, when,
finally, it began to come in his second year, first with
cricket and then with his use of the native language, had
a sour edge to it, as if the dearly won applause was con-
ceded grudgingly. But here was Maurice, *touching* him in
that part of his self that was most secret, an Englishman
whose hand had played about his thighs, undone the
buttons and drawn out his penis and held it with pleasure, beginning to stroke it gently, before swallowing
the remaining sherry in his glass, placing the glass on
the ground, slipping off the sofa and turning around on
his knees to bring himself between Max's legs. At the
last moment, before he lowered his lips for a preliminary kiss expressive of adoration and also gratitude that
he could take such a gift without objection, Maurice
looked up and his eyes caught Max staring at him but,
of course, did not notice the complicated knot of shock

and triumph, loathing and yearning tightened in that gaze, for Max wanted nothing more than to push the debauched face away, to kick it and stamp upon it, while at the same time wanting to hold it strongly in his hands and make certain that he did not flinch from opening his mouth and swallowing whole his penis until, looking down, he saw nothing but the curly black pubic hairs against the blond head.

Entranced in that dream of a wealthy future, sometimes you walk past Adam and Eve Mews, possessed by a fantasy that, scorning the recent acquisitions in the High Street shops as too modest, has outfitted you in a Jermyn Street shirt, a Savile Row suit and hand-made boots from Air Street, and you snap out of vanity's gleaming vision only at the traffic lights at Earls Court Road across from the gate to Holland Park next to the modern, so-called, building of the Commonwealth Institute. Fanciful all those flags of the Commonwealth nations, how petty and worthless such pomp, big pompous shell the Commonwealth Institute for artsy-crafty folkloric displays and scholarly seminars on hot sub-Saharan winds of change. You wait for the light to turn green. Sharpesville massacre, cannibal dictators, and what other horrors, O God, Kashmir for one, Biafra another, and all this pious humbug about the community of nations and fat women in native costumes that no native wears any longer selling folkloric trinkets in Kensington like

there was nothing but peace and happiness in the bloody
Commonwealth. Green at last. You cross the street, turn
your eyes to the green gloom of Holland Walk behind
the open gate to the park. Nice little cricket ground
there. Short boundary. *Tock*, there goes a six. Never
played there, though. Young couple with backpacks striding up Holland Walk. That purposeful Nordic stride,
walking or cross-country skiing the same thing for those
legs. Youth hostel up there in the park. Beyond that the
squash court. Play there with Stannie some Sundays, go
to a pub afterwards. The Prince of Wales up the little
street from the corner of Norland Square. Another time,
not past, not to come. They have money, Max and
Stannie in that time not past, not to come, and have
bought a bottle of claret, so there's a date on the label,
good vintage year. Max brings out a folded sheet of paper
from the breast pocket of his old college blazer and
spreads it open on the little table and places the bottle
at its top right corner. The ruled sheet of paper is headed,
Stannie's Film Treatment. Number one, says Max, this
opening sequence, forget the Dali clock, I think, and
that pun showing a woman's face with nervous tics at
the corners of her eyes and then a couple of ticks sucking
the blood at her cheeks, I don't know, too clever by half
to work, I think, beware of symbols that wink at the
audience. But it's better, says Stannie, than showing
flowers on a sundial withering in a time-lapse sequence,
besides I want that incubus suggestion. Then let her be

asleep, says Max, and let the demon lover come to her and suck her blood, show the teeth marks on her bosom fair. The madness, the horror, says Stannie, staring into his glass, which are neither real nor surreal. Precisely, says Max, therefore no Dali quotation, no Buñuel touch, subterranean or submarine the image you need for that timeless love, the hair flowing like seaweed in green liquid luminosity and then spring that shock, the breast bitten into by the demon lover, a crab scuttling across her belly and plopping upon the mons veneris. Talk of winking symbols! says Stannie, and adds, Only if it were so, the ocean depth drumming its pressure in one's ear. Number two, says Max, the counter theme of the unfaithful female, scrap the idea of dressing her in a Chinese jacket and trendy Biba trousers to suggest she's no less independent than a man. She's of this time, says Stannie, fiercely feminist. But, says Max, that's not why she's unfaithful, ideology's not the poison her whole blood stream fills. Ah yes, says Stannie, smiling at the recollection of the familiar villanelle and seeing that Max is about to speak aloud its famous line, joins in the recitation, *The waste remains, the waste remains and kills.* The two raise their glasses and drink. The landlord behind the counter just then pulling a pint of beer for a mustachioed gentleman in a black and brown hound's tooth sports jacket and cavalry twill trousers looks past the customer's shoulder at the two young men, allows the muscles of his face to twitch slightly to express his

disapproval of their stentorian outburst and, satisfied
that they have themselves in control, continues to draw
the beer with his usual unhurried serenity. Number
three, says Max, interesting all that fast cutting from
scene to scene, good that shot of the red Ferrari with the
British racing green Vanwall on its tail at Silverstone,
quick flash down the fast track, cut, the Vanwall making
a pit-stop, cut, close-up of stopwatch and a thumb clicking time in motion, cut, Vanwall taking off in hot pursuit, cut, close-up of thumb clicking to stop time, eleven
seconds lost, cut, out of the Formula One world in
bright exterior light and suddenly inside a subdued interior a woman's head against a pillow partly concealed by
the back of a man's head, cut, the Vanwall and the Ferrari
roar up to a corner side by side, cut, a man's back with a
woman's arms clasped round it, her tense fingers making
depressions in his flesh, cut, the Ferrari coming out of
the corner in a ferocious four-wheel drift inches ahead
of the Vanwall, cut . . . , when Stannie puts up a hand
and says, There's nothing in the script about the fingers
making indentations. You're bound to hit on details
when you start shooting, says Max, the present moment
always has a spontaneous unscripted suggestion to make,
but what I like is that all that fast cutting is in footage
that will take perhaps three minutes of screen time, if
that, and is followed by an almost still shot held longer
on the screen of the man alone in bed in the pose of *The
Death of Chatterton*. But naked, says Stannie. But naked,

repeats Max. Naked and detumescent, says Stannie. I'm
glad we see no more of what happened at Silverstone,
says Max, no happy or tragic ending, no Vanwall nosing
ahead at the finish or Ferrari losing a wheel and plough-
ing into the crowd, something happened for a time, perhaps, or nothing happened, possibly, a scam set up by
the mind to entrap some fantasy, that's all, a fragment of
a story entered one's consciousness and vanished, that's
all, there was no motor-racing imagery earlier, there'll be
none later, the fast images just crashed into one's consciousness for a minute or two and vanished, that's all,
no symbols intended. A woman, beautiful and young,
says Stannie, in a long skirt and high-collared blouse,
firmly corseted, parasol open above her head, riding a
penny-farthing on the front at Brighton, could splice
that in somewhere, a touch of sentimental Victoriana,
keep up the beloved myth of a bygone age we so miss.
And then, says Max, a shell falling on a trench, a huge
explosion, shattered fragments rain down. Stannie looks
at him, his eyes startled and then sad, and says, Cut to
a man, haggard and homeless with wrinkled female dugs
scavenging in the rubbish on Hell's Mouth beach in
Wales, a touch of the modern waste land, *These fragments
I have shored against my ruins*. Take it underwater from
there for the final sequence, says Max, forget about the
rain falling on black umbrellas, dive into the dark water
again and follow the mysterious black fish in the coral's
labyrinth, cut for a quick second to a close-up of a

woman's bare thigh as she rolls over in bed, cut back to the disappearing fish, pan across dark water and stop at image of a bone on the ocean's floor, rolling very gently as if the passing black fish had generated a little current. Stannie looks at Max suspiciously, not sure if there's not some irony behind his suggestion, and says, No symbol intended, I suppose? Why, none at all, says Max, the ocean's littered with bones, nothing could be more literal. Full fathom five. Ah well, says Stannie, not fully convinced, but nevertheless feels compelled to add, They are pearls that were his eyes. The bottle is empty. Stannie picks it up and turns it upside down with its neck over Max's glass. After a long moment, a drop forms on the bottle's lip, hesitates there and finally falls into the glass. Max looks at the date on the label. Good vintage year that. Upside down, the year records the same date as it did when the bottle was upright. Determined to press on that Nordic couple surely making for the youth hostel at the top of Holland Park, why Nordic, could be Australians for all you know, same vigorous type out to see everything in the world. Looks pleasantly cool, Holland Walk, the air must be fresher there, without these fumes, this oily smell. Must get a good view of the park from those flats. Tops of the trees, an undulating green on a breezy summer's day, and in the winter branches like broom-ends, thrashing the air. Exhilarating it must be, to look down on the park, not to notice it much of the time but suddenly in some moment that flickers in the mind as a puzzling vision to experience an inexplicable enchantment, an obscure comprehension of the beauty of things. Thinner the crowd this side of the High Street. You've walked too far and have to make up time, not that Brenda will mind, you never know if she's pleased when you're early or annoyed when you're late.

When you're just about to go past St Mary Abbots into Church Street you see that the bus, at last freed from the bottleneck before Barker's, is making for the stop opposite the old library where you would be jumping off the running board at this moment, so you've neither gained nor lost time, that's how it often happens, it comes to the same in the end, you would have smoked a cigarette sitting in the bus, instead your lungs are full of traffic fumes, same thing, nothing's gained. The air smells of diesel, making you faintly nauseous. From the church tower there's a frenzy of bells, hard to tell why so much ringing all of a sudden, the clock's hands are neither at the hour nor at one of its quarters, no wedding, baptism or funeral that you can tell, only a frenzied tolling, but the throngs on the pavement walk past not even looking at the church and no one is sent to ask why all that urgent tolling. But it stops as suddenly as it had begun and you are at Brenda's door, your ear listening for the remote tinkle in her flat which she might not hear, as has happened before, because the chime of the doorbell coincided with her placing a pan on the stove or running water at the sink or tuning the radio from the Third Programme to the Light, and you press the button again to make sure the doorbell has rung and listening intently think you can hear her footsteps and imagine her barefooted, though of course she will not be, only a line has come to your mind, *With naked foot stalking within my chamber*, and imagining her thus you imagine too the curving arch of her right instep that you often trace with a forefinger, commencing at her foot a slow climb upon her flesh. Glossy black the paint on the door, faintly reflected on it a silhouette of your head, your hand at the bell, the index finger pressing once more the white button in the middle of the polished brass ring when there's a jolt in the atmosphere, for suddenly have resumed their tumultuous tolling the bells of St Mary Abbots, but just then the mirror is pulled away and where had been your head is Brenda's face and in the second before you enter you look at her body clad in a navy blue jumper and grey skirt and in that moment she raises her left foot to scratch the right calf and you are surprised to see the foot embedded in the moss green carpet is naked, and in a retrospective and backward completion, *They flee from me*, the words come to your mind, *that sometime did me seek*.

II

What is this space between myself and myself?

Fernando Pessoa, *The Book of Disquiet.*

THEN THERE IS the fourth, not you, on overcast days, not a shadow of his, in the grey midday light, in the cold sharp breeze of November, not I taking long breaths under the silver birches of Putney Heath, not you, not he, not I, in that shadowless abstraction of autumnal grey next to the desolate cricket ground where one summer afternoon he swept the ball off his front foot and sent it sailing over the boundary rope into the ferny wood, in the Heath with its ghostly silver birches, but who is the fourth who sees everything everywhere, an eye like a little planet orbiting where I am, and again I am not, a presence in the darkest part of the wood where one knows one is being watched though there's no one to be seen, not a foot snapping a twig or a warm breath puffing out as a tiny cloud in the cold air, yet there is the fourth who lurks like a voyeur behind a chestnut tree in Parliament Hill Fields, the shadow of his hat slowly sliding from behind the trunk, there's the stealthy slow motion of a body slipping behind the bushes like a stalker, and whose those footsteps on the dry fallen leaves of the plane trees in St James's, no one to be seen when I look back, and that silhouette of the figure on

the bridge, like a spy in a film feigning anonymity as if
he would be invisible, on the Serpentine bridge, gazing
out at the Long Water at the thrashing branches of the
willow tree, who everywhere in London is the perpetually
present fourth where I am, and again I am not, and even
on warm blue summer days under the cool of the black
poplars on the towpath past Hammersmith, now your
shadow hard-edged where the bright July sun throws it
on the dry ground, a female jogger running past, quietly,
as if breath were unnecessary, flowing past like the river's
current, a film of sweat on her white arms, the limbs
silvery like the river, and I see her jump over your
shadow, there is the fourth there, too, where the brightness is so intense nothing can be seen, but he steps aside
to make room for a middle-aged man in a cloth cap with
a black Labrador on a leash, the dog straining the length
of leather and forcing long, eager strides from the man,
there is a witness present as if the knots on the poplar
trunks were eyes or the washed pebbles on the water's
edge were lenses with shutter speed set for a time-lapse
sequence, the river softly ebbing, forming a little muddy
beach the colour of molasses, run, sweet Thames, run,
run, run, where I am, and again I am not. How often
you coming up the steps from the District Line at South
Ken see him standing opposite the news-stand in the
arcade where commuters in their eternal haste stride past
and I am surprised, and again I am not, at his statue's
patience waiting there scanning the flow of faces to see

if one does not suddenly transform to hers, who, oh
Jenny Byrne or Mirabel or the one as yet nameless, some
current conviction of love posited by desire, and for a
moment I am again there in his expectant and apprehensive state of mind, though outwardly calm, standing
like a plainclothes policeman unobtrusively inspecting
the passing faces, looking to match the composite form
of beauty already assembled in his mind, Jenny's or
Mirabel's or the one as yet nameless . . . *If ever any beauty
I did see* . . . her face elusive because looked for . . .
Which I desired, and got . . . solid as an illusion, her face,
because not there, present for an instant in every passing
female face . . . *'twas but a dream of thee* . . . a hopeful
montage compiled by expectation and desire, within the
frame of each female who floated across the arcade the
form of the one as yet nameless, the rumble and the
squeak and skirr of the District Line in the background
constant then and now, still. Sod it, says Stannie, sulking
over his pint in the Chelsea Potter, his pale cheeks sag-
ging, his mood sour, the rattle of glasses, the hiss of beer
being drawn, clouds of cigarette smoke, the buzz and
roar of voices, sudden guffaws of laughter, sod the snobs,
sod the EtonHarrow cunts, he sips his beer and swallows
a mouthful of expletives, then goes down to the Gents
and comes back revived, refurbished like one returning
from a tailor in a new suit, he talks of the dome of St
Paul's seen through a gap between buildings, an image
of the constant presence of things suddenly encountered

when one had thought them absent or had forgotten
them and there, in the gap, they unexpectedly appeared,
filling one with surprise and sorrow, as if the mind asked
why should it think of her now but, having thought, the
space presumed empty framed her face, O sod it, he
says, relapsing into his sulk, and starts to curse the whole
world, Sod the pricks at Ascot in their top hats, Sod the
cunts at Cheltenham, and on and on he goes in a foul-
mouthed, arse-kicking rejection of society, but curses
not the lady who left him, only finally heaves a huge sigh
and picks up the glass to swallow what's left of the pint
in one annoyed jerk of his neck, and I think he straightened his tie for nothing when he'd gone down to the
Gents, perhaps it was an unconscious habit, to put a
hand to the knot. Come now to Cheyne Walk, no longer
on the corner there the Pier Hotel where with her on a
two-seat sofa by the fire-place in the saloon bar you
warmed your blood with whisky and soda, demolished,
eliminated that space, stroll up Beaufort Street to the
pub on the corner with King's Road where on a spring
evening with her you sat sipping gin and tonic but it's a
French restaurant now, not that old pub with the
Watney's sign, demolished, eliminated that space, stroll
down Chelsea Embankment where your arms round her
waist you leaned against the thick stone wall in the misty
October night with the lights on Albert Bridge casting
oddly a gloom and not illumination on the dark river,
still there that stone wall, but when you stroll down

Chelsea Embankment you walk softly past away from the wall as if lovers leaned there against each other, motionless, cast in bronze, eternal their embrace, below them the river jostling up the embankment with the incoming tide and slowly ebbing out to sea, constantly, come now to Battersea Park, an afternoon of sunny spells and long periods of grey, cool gusts of the wind swirling down from the swaying trees in early May, scattering hawthorn blossom like powdery snow on the path, there installed in the sculpture garden among forms of stone and steel whose organic mystery makes them appear weightless like phantoms floating in the air is the heavy monumental presence that yet is fluid and continually shifting that you had not expected to see there, for apparitions vanish, do they not, but here installed is the obelisk self, you look and are overwhelmed by its colossal mass but when, with the hawthorn blossoms blowing across your eyes, you blink for a second and look again, it's gone, but only to appear behind you, though just when you're convinced it's there, it's not, but then what is the shadow falling before you of a long column, and just when you're going to swivel quickly round the wind does a sonic boom dive through the trees and there's so much hawthorn blossom blowing into your eyes you could be stranded in a blizzard. In a tube station some distance from the centre, Archway perhaps, one with shops, an arcade of shops, in a small bookshop full of second-hand books, nineteenth-century and early

twentieth-century leather-bound volumes, English Prize,
History Prize, names of winning scholars, William
Arbuthnot, Oliver Prescott, or a list of boys in the same
class in successive terms written in ink gone brown on
the flyleaf of the Golden Treasury, a dusty bookshop
where a thin bearded man in a dark grey cardigan reading in a corner behind a desk ignores the two men
browsing, you pick up a volume of Herbert, clean gold-
stamped the title on the smooth leather spine, 4/- lightly
pencilled on the inside, you know you have a florin and
a half-crown, two threepenny bits and some coppers in
your pocket but still you put your hand in and feel the
milling on the two silver coins to make sure you have the
money, and walk to the bearded man and silently give
him the two coins and he silently gives you six pence
without even looking to see the price of the book and
dropping the six pence among the pennies in the pocket
you walk out Herbert in hand, your fingertips happy
caressing the leather, and going to buy your ticket you
know you have enough for the fare only as far as South
Ken and from there you will have a four-mile walk
home, but you knew that already when you took the
two silver coins out and gave them to the bearded man
and he did not even look at you and you, receiving the
six pence in your outstretched hand, had your eyes on
the second button of his cardigan which was hanging
loose. Archway, what was he doing in Archway, walked
down Highgate Hill probably or was waiting for a bus

to go up Highgate Hill and something caught his eye in
the arcade in Archway, up Highgate Hill, whatever for,
to get to Highgate, why else would anyone go up
Highgate Hill, but what would he have done when he
got up Highgate Hill, go see a woman, what else, you
dope, what other reason can there be for a young man
to go up Highgate Hill if not to reach Highgate and see
a woman, you really are thick sometimes, plain stupid
if you ask me, come off it, this is the first time you men-
tioned Highgate, who was there in Highgate, you've
been going on and on about Brenda in Kensington
Church Street without ever getting there, either into her
flat or into her skirt, and now it's Highgate Hill and
Archway of all places and I'm the stupid one not to con-
nect that with some bird, well, I did mention Grace, but
that was Holloway Road, and where do you think
Archway is, just up the road from Holloway Road, and
if you want to go to Parliament Hill Fields from there
what do you do but take a bus and go up Highgate Hill,
unless you want to walk but it's pretty steep, to Highgate
and cut across from there to Parliament Hill Fields from
where you can see the city, Dick Whittington's London
Town, St Paul's and everything, and where there was that
thicket Grace had led him to and led inside, if you know
what I mean, some good old houses there, in Highgate,
big mansion types some of them with the nose of a Jag
3.8 sticking out of the drive that had our friend thinking
that perhaps his future was not in Launceton Place but

just off Highgate High Street, that house with a walled
garden with the Jag peeping out, and this question,
whether he should alter the conditions of his affluent
future from Kensington to Highgate became a mathematical problem in his brain each time he walked from
where the bus dropped him in Highgate to the entrance
to Parliament Hill Fields, how much more money he'd
need, for there was this new question of the car which
he could do without in Launceton Place but was a neces-
sity in Highgate and which would have to be a Jag, the
new E-Type obviously, a problem that was further aggra-
vated by the consideration that if he lived in Highgate
then how was he going to get to Kensington Gardens,
why would he want to go there if he's in Highgate and
Hampstead Heath is round the corner, why do you insist
on asking stupid questions, nothing stupid about that,
just practical, a park is a park, green is green, why not
Hampstead Heath if you're living in Highgate, because
there's a mad stubbornness in him, or call it an obsession,
a fixation, a mania, a bloody passion to go strolling down
the Flower Walk in Kensington Gardens whatever the
weather or the season, so it worried him, this bit of math-
ematics he had to juggle in his mind each time he got off
the bus in Highgate, that answers it then, what. There is
a flower-bed in Regent's Park, I cannot say where, with
a short iron railing the height of croquet hoops around
it, where we entered, I do not know how, after the park
had closed, Mirabel and I, she tall and fair, the only

perfume on her the odour of her sex, dark and wintry the night, little drifts of fog loitering palely in the orangish light from the distant street lamps, strong her legs striding with me, supple the feel of her hip against my eager leg, the two of us walking as if we had a fixed destination in mind, and coming to the flower-bed which had been turned up for the winter, in a quick synchronised movement, as if previously rehearsed, we stepped over the railing and I spread my coat upon the ground, and afterwards I thought that everything that happened with Mirabel happened as if it had been previously rehearsed, all the happiness and misery and the drama had occurred between us long before we met and, I do not know why, even long before she was born, but that night rising from the ground we stepped lightly away from the flower-bed, springing childishly over the railing, and looking back to see what impression we had left in the earth. Ask him about the grove down the slope in Parliament Hill Fields where the land comes down as two thighs and there's a bushy thicket in the middle concavity, ask him the names of the trees in their solitary splendour on the hill's crown, ask him to stop inhaling the yeasty smell rising from the moist earth still wet from the afternoon rain, ask him to put his hands to his ears and not listen to the swish-swish of the grass, ask him not to imagine it was the nightingale's song he had heard, ask him, ask him. Clive faces St James's Park, high on his pedestal, his back to the Foreign Office, to

Whitehall, pleased, if he could know it, to have his arse
to the Commons, more agreeable the view of the tops of
trees, more pleasing the song of thrushes, more musical
even the quack-quack of mallards than the engravings in
the picture-book of revisionist history, amused perhaps
by the glimpse of the palace from whose balcony peri-
odically wave arms braceleted with diamonds from his
India, Clive, serene above the forgetful crowd, who, sailing out for Madras and then Bengal was cast by the
winds against Pernambuco and then Rio de Janeiro, and
secured for England the imperial passage for her bejewelled crown, a name now on a pedestal for incurious
tourists, but you, coming to the park one June evening
with her, in a lyrical mood after the opera, humming
the Nabucco chorus, see Clive's dark silhouette against
the light summer night, and as you hasten away towards
the plane trees above the farther bank of the little lake,
you feel his eyes look down and follow your steps on a
patch of his green England and though you sing aloud
a line from the chorus, and she beside you in a softer
voice, other words are being heard in your head and you
reassure him, Yes, you say, you were the master of India,
No, no, he says, it is not to glory that I refer, Plunder,
then, you say, the fabled treasures of the East, Not that
neither, he says, Not forgetting, you add, the Brazilian
gold that Portugal spent in London, All that for what,
he says sadly, parties of school children pass below me
to go look at the animals on Horse Guards Parade, but

you are now repeating the chorus, and she beside you is louder too, and you fling yourself on the grass under a plane tree and she falls upon you, crushing you against the little patch of green. 1964 and the summer is warm and bright and endless, it seems everyone is young, the girls are called birds and wear mini-skirts that become so short there's only a nine-inch wide strip encircling the hips, golden legs on the pavement of High Street Ken, in and out of Biba's, at last the grey that had fallen over London in the war years has been washed away, the houses in Onslow Square are brilliant white, their doors red or purple or black, the railing round the square tipped with gold, This is our time, this is our decade, everyone says, and everyone is young, there's a new music with its loud pulse throbbing from the new stereo systems, there's a popular happiness on black and white television sets, no more that grandiloquent BBC voice but echoes from the streets of Liverpool or the speech of Hull, a line of Tridents and Caravelles and Boeing 707s continuously descend upon London, the young of the world have heard of King's Road and Carnaby Street, consume and dispose is the consensus, make it cheap, make it quick, wear it and throw it away, That Was the Week That Was, goodbye to it, make a joke of it and let it go, everyone is in a hurry, and everyone is young, you sit in the Partisan café where there's talk of a classless society, but on another day you are in El Vino's among journalists drinking champagne and one says, Here's to swinging London, but there in the centre there is no movement, from the centre of the great carousel sitting among journalists who invent present reality you watch the swinging periphery, bright and colourful, but on another day you are a guest in the Athenaeum eating pheasant and drinking claret where old men seem to have fallen into an eternal somnolence in leather chairs as if history itself had collapsed in an exhausted heap and the past was no more than a dream they had once had and coming out and walking up Regent's Street you find the present explode again, all relevance to the old men's dream kicked away by the mini-skirted legs in the gorgeous gaiety of the present, and you cut across Air Street into Soho and amble past the strip joints and up Old Compton Street and end up again in the Partisan where the phrases about the classless society mingle with the cigarette smoke, but on another day you are in Sweeting's with a publisher, drinking Chablis with your Dover sole, the fortune of his house built upon the history of the mind and interpretations of its dreams, the anthropology of the self, propositions whereof we may speak or remain silent, he's thinking of becoming a dealer in rare books, he says, the entrapped past in old leather binding, he knows of collectors he can depend upon, people who want to possess and finger the past, there are two or three of them still he can count on to be steady clients whose pulse quickens when they touch an old book, outside around Bank there's a bustle of young men and the

criss-crossing of mini-skirted legs on the pavement has-
tening with messages from the Stock Exchange, everyone is in a hurry, and everyone is young, the Monument
is deserted, a clatter of footsteps on the pavement in
Lombard Street above the basement of banks where
clerks correspond with foreign branches, transmitting
long columns of numbers, profit and loss, For Your
Immediate Attention. But on another day you are in the
French pub in Soho listening to Stannie's nouvelle vague
enthusiasm, he wants to make films, he says, if the moneyed sods will let him, and you watch whole scenes in
his watery blue eyes, sequences in which an improbable
assemblage and juxtaposition of disparate images appear
perfectly natural, astonishing forms become familiar, the
novelty of art is only an initial provocation to capture
the viewer's amazed attention, for even the surreal in the
end is composed of banal reality, O there's a whole new
cinema in Stannie's watery blue eyes, you see reels of film
winding about his head like a turban, but he gets no
answers from the moneyed sods, and you walk with him
to Better Books and then down Charing Cross Road,
stopping to look into Zwemmer's, then past the second-hand bookshops, complete editions of Dickens in
blue or red or green cloth binding in the windows, you
wander into Leicester Square where there is a long queue
of mini-skirts and bell-bottom trousers outside the
Gaumont for an American film, but on another day. And
then the surprise of the city from the distant hills, a

silhouetted panorama on the horizon, blurred grey edges
when heavy clouds hang low, St Paul's a smudge left on
a window-pane by a child's thumb, all the streets you
walked, sometimes jauntily with a da-dum da-dum vocal
accompaniment and sometimes in a silent scansion of
the pavement, compressed in that view—once many
years after you had left the city and were on a trans-At-
lantic flight to Europe you were surprised the Lufthansa
747 flew right over London and from the window at
seat 33A on that bright cloudless morning you could see
all of the city in one astonished glance, like an exile
being shown an aerial shot of his home town, and as if
you held a magnifying lens over a detail you pointed,
Look!, for never was vision so amazed by clarity, that's
St Peter's Church next to the Great West Road, I can
even see that silly statue of a woman in an improbable
pose, her leaning body unsupported and so out of bal-
ance someone once stuck a broom between her elbow
and the ground, and look, Kensington Gardens and
Hyde Park, how clear everything is, and you see him
walking those streets in his unceasing curiosity of what
the city would disclose past the next corner, and seeing
it all in one glance you cannot tell if that time is not now
and you are not he, those years when he and London,
so he believed, were inseparable, there was a London
only he knew who walked once from Vauxhall to
Richmond Hill, but in this view of that whole now with
only a cartographical projection of parks and landmarks

and not one person visible, from the window at seat 33A at 30,000 feet and when you look around the cabin everyone else is asleep, it is as if an illusion had been contrived only for you, a London where the plane does not touch down but is exclusively yours for this eternal moment which at nearly 500 miles per hour lasts scarcely a minute, for look, there's Tower Bridge now, now already passed, the river widens, and far to the north, in the English Channel, thick smoke is rising from a barge, burning the city's waste.

III

We know no time when we were not as now.

John Milton, *Paradise Lost*.

CONSPICUOUS IN HIS recollection, though scarcely observed at the time, there was an apple tree in the garden below Brenda's first-floor bedroom that briefly caught Max's attention when he saw her rise out of bed and after drawing back the curtain stand a moment by the window observing the tree's swaying branches and vaguely registering the change in the weather from a calm morning to a blustery afternoon. Max remained in bed, his back pressed against two pillows and head against the wall, and lit a cigarette. He caught a glimpse of the branches as a sudden gust of wind swung them across the window where, were the air still, he would not have seen them. He was about to remark that the tree must be very pretty in the spring and perhaps she ought to rearrange the bed in the room so that one could see the tree without having to raise oneself to an uncomfortable position, but silently smoked his cigarette, realising that the remark would make no impression on Brenda's brain since having for about half an hour remained passively receptive in bed her demeanour was that of one who now had pressing work to do. He watched her, his eyes drawn in the suddenly increased light to a gleaming film of moisture on her calves just below the grey skirt that swirled when she turned back from the window. She plucked a navy-blue jumper from a chair and quickly put it over the light blue blouse that she had already buttoned up. There was a deliberate quickness in her movements whenever she got out of bed, as if she had overslept and needed to make up for lost time, and to Max she always looked as though she had done her duty, lain in bed with him for half an hour, permitting a warm intimacy, letting his fingers unbutton her blouse or caress her softly from a foot to an inner thigh, raising up her skirt as if incidentally, but she held his wrist tightly and thrust his hand away if he attempted to go further, making sure that both of them remained clothed even when she let him lie upon her and pushed eagerly in a mock intercourse until he seemed spent, and, her duty done, she jumped out of bed. He sucked at his cigarette, watching her pick up the tea tray from a small table, and though her lips looked swollen, even bruised, from being pressed hard between his and the colour at her cheeks was a faint shade darker and indicated at least a slight agitation if not a tumult within her blood set off by an irrepressible passion, her dreamy eyes, the eye-lids falling heavily over them, suggested she had just risen from a deep sleep and not from her lover's embrace. The cigarette-end had become wet and he took it away from his mouth and crushed the cigarette in the ashtray. He saw her walk out of the room to go to the adjoining kitchenette, watched her grey skirt's shiver and swing in response to the movement of her buttocks. A gust of wind suddenly rattled the window and Max caught another glimpse of the top of the apple tree, its branches shaking confusedly as if a flock of finches had just descended on the tree and competed on the tops of the branches for foothold. He heard water running in the kitchenette. Brenda was rinsing the tea cups, then washing out the tea pot. She hated to see unclean things left on a table or counter top. If they ate together, she had to get the washing-up done as soon as they finished, else she remained distracted and fidgety. Earlier, sitting on the edge of the bed, drinking tea, his taking the opportunity when she put her cup down to lean his face to hers and then push her back into the bed had prevented her from marching out to the kitchenette with the tea tray. Hearing her determinedly proceed with the washing up, sending the spoons clattering against the counter top, made him wonder whether during the half hour she had lain in his embrace her only thought had been the distressing one of the dirty tea cups in the tray on the little table, or that, in the lover's anticipated possession of a woman's loveliness, when he whispered with wet lips against her breast his joy at her body, whether instead of her own radiant beauty being willingly surrendered the image in her mind was not of tea leaves at the bottom of a cup polluting her emotions with a lingering disgust with untidiness. No, it could not be,

he concluded, she was not that alien to the arousal of
desire, for had she not, when he had manoeuvred her
to her side and had succeeded in burying his face in her
bosom and then managed to probe his tongue into the
cleavage, repeatedly entering and withdrawing from the
tight but cushiony passage there, his saliva creating a
warm wetness between the compressed breasts, had she
not been overcome then by a sudden flaring of desire that
made her manipulate her bra to let her whole breast spill
out and when he quickly fastened his lips on the nipple
did not a sigh escape from her mouth? Another gust of
wind and the tops of the apple tree's branches shuddered,
giving him a momentary glimpse of tiny green apples
on a branch. A cabinet door was heard to close in the
kitchenette—Brenda putting away the tin of digestive
biscuits. Heaving up her chest, she had assisted him to
free her other breast when his mouth let go the first nipple and sought its twin, and his head remained there in
a confusion of blouse, bra and a sheet that Brenda had
pulled over them, his breath hot upon her breast, saliva
oozing out of his mouth upon her nipple, in that partial darkness in which only his agitated blood perceived
naked flesh, for her whole body, never at once revealed,
was a fantasy in his vision, he saw her and held her only
in fragments. He slid a hand down her stomach and
slipped it beneath an obstructing elastic band and was
thrilled to be stroking wiry hair. Again a sigh escaped
Brenda's lips and she pushed up quickly, rapidly, four

or five times. He was encouraged to tug at the elastic to pull the garment down but at that moment she grasped his wrist and held his hand away from her legs. He raised himself to lie upon her, and though she snatched up the sheet and drew it across her waist as he did so, and in any case he had his trousers on, she thrust back when he pressed upon her, held him tightly and eagerly opened her mouth when his tongue parted her lips, thrust back harder and more rapidly, until she felt him throb, go tense and then fall into a swoon. She went slack, suddenly far removed from desire. He lay beside her, on his side, slowly regaining his breath, a hand tightly fisted at the trouser front, feeling a spreading wetness inside his underpants. His eyes closed, he could yet see she was quickly rearranging her clothes, pulling at the bra straps, buttoning the blouse, rubbing across the creases. Soon she had leapt out of the bed as if the phone was ringing in the hall below and she had to rush to get it. He wondered if what he had been impressed to believe was an irrepressible eruption of desire when she held him tightly and pushed up frenziedly in a mimicry of intercourse had not been a counterfeit performance put on to hasten his falling into a state of exhaustion.

The noise in the kitchenette ceased and he saw her returning, a contented serenity on her face. 'Come and sit down,' he said, patting the edge of the mattress, but she took the chair at the foot of the bed instead, in front of the window, and he asked, 'Why so distant, come where I can look into your eyes.' She glanced out the window at the swaying tops of the apple tree's branches and said, 'Yvonne and Wendy just came back.' Max had not heard the front door, its opening and closing must have coincided with Brenda's noisy washing up, but the voices of the two young women who shared the flat with Brenda were now audible from the ground floor. 'This is your room, he said, 'they're not going to come barging in.' 'We ought to join them,' she answered, 'it's impolite to ignore them.' 'Christ, Brenda, you're not living with your parents, why should you worry what Yvonne and Wendy think? Besides we're not doing anything, only talking.' 'They won't know that,' she replied, 'and anyway Mark and Andy are coming for high tea.' 'Don't tell me you offered to help in their kitchen,' he spoke a little sharply, 'all Yvonne does is open a tin of baked beans while Wendy makes the toast, which she invariably burns, but you've got to be everyone's mum and kill yourself in the kitchen baking a cake, what's it going to be, pineapple upside down again?' She remained silent, her face shadowed with resentment at his anger. 'I see,' he continued when she had not spoken for a minute, 'it is going to be pineapple upside down. Really, Brenda, sometimes I think you worry more about feeding Mark and Andy than you care for me.' 'That's unfair!' she said with some warmth. 'Nonsense,' he countered, 'you're going to spend hours in the kitchen while I sit here staring out at the apple tree.' 'You could do the decent

thing,' she suggested, 'and go and talk with Mark and
Andy.' '*Decent* thing! How very nicely domestic, you
slave away in the kitchen while the men sit smoking and
talking about football, just what your feminist sisters
think women are fit for!'

'O Max,' she said, 'why are you being so difficult?'
'Not difficult at all, Brenda, it's very simple, I come to
be with you, to hold you, to love you.' 'There's a time
for everything,' she said almost in a whisper, as if weary
of arguing with him, but then, her voice suddenly sharp
with accusation, 'But you want only . . . *that*.' 'That
what?' he demanded, 'you can't even bring yourself to
utter the word *sex*.' She surprised him then by rising out
of the chair, quickly coming to the edge of the bed and
flinging her arms round his neck. She kissed him and
then pressing her cheek to his, her mouth near his left
ear, said, 'I love you too much for that.'

Her statement so astonished him that he pushed her
back a little to look into her eyes, wanting to say that she
was being absurd, for how could anyone feel so much
love as to reject love's ultimate objective, the elimina-
tion of confrontation and the union of opposites in a
moment's absolute merging of two identities into one
with such force that in that moment of suspended time
neither retained an awareness of its own self, but a dullness had settled in her eyes and he realised that what he
perceived to be an expression of dreaminess appeared
more to be one of vacuity, and he remained silent. Who

had devised such a grossly idealised concept of love that it could exist only in some ethereal realm, unconnected with the reality of human flesh? As if, by jealously guarding its chaste wholeness and protecting itself from extraneous pollution, the self remained in a state of pure existence in which it discovered a supreme ecstasy through unrelenting physical denial. Fast and pray, mortify the body, draw blood upon your flesh with flagellation, and you will be filled with the love of God. Get thee to a nunnery, go! Very likely some bureaucracy of priests had first broadcast the notion that sex was dirty and, by association, words denoting the sexual organs were dirty words, and pictures depicting naked bodies were dirty pictures. More than merely an emptiness, there was in her eyes, now that Max stared at them without seeing them as dreamy, that look of puzzlement and incomprehension that comes over a congregation when it does not hear an affirmation of those dogma which it believes to be unshakable truths but is obliged instead to listen to some challenging thought. He had been under no illusion about the quality of her intellect but had suppressed his negative evaluation of it, being driven by the egotistical male's obsession with sexual conquest, but now perceived what a futile pursuit that was when the person was an intellectual nonentity. Seeing his eyes fixed for so long upon hers, and interpreting in his look a hint of sympathy, even of admiration, for what she had said, she kissed him quickly on the mouth and again pressing her cheek to his, repeated in his ear, what she took to be a successful, and unanswerable, formula, 'I love you too much for that.'

He was seized by an ambiguous impulse, to push her aside and make a quick and permanent exit from her life, or to turn her on her back and force himself upon her. If only he had held on to the idea of her eyes being dreamy, he might have continued to put together in his imagination the several parts of her person that he had seen separately exposed and continued—in that charming naïveté of entertaining a romantic fantasy— to imagine the full loveliness of female form of which the complete revelation was worth waiting for, but now that he saw her eyes as dull, as organs attached to an undeveloped brain providing it with a blurry evidence of received ideas, her mind storing the highlighted clichés of common convention as if they constituted essential wisdom, he was suddenly overwhelmed by a weariness with her world. 'You're right, Brenda,' he said softly, gently pushing her back, and she, not hearing the note of sad resignation in his voice, rose quickly from the bed, saying, 'You were right, pet, it is going to be a pineapple upside down cake', and did not see him wince on imagining himself her poodle.

He heard Yvonne and Wendy shrieking with laughter when he was tidying himself in the upstairs bathroom and on joining them a few minutes later in the front sitting room found them in that state when people have

exhausted themselves laughing at a joke but no sooner
do they recover their seriousness when a memory of
the joke makes them burst out once more and it is only
after a succession of little eruptions of laughter and gig-
gles that they recover full seriousness. A white blind
had been pulled down on the window that looked out
to the street, more to keep the intermittent sunlight
out of the front room than to prevent the occasional
passer-by from looking in, and the joke was that when
Mark and Andy had arrived a few minutes ago they
had seized the opportunity of the sun just then shining
brightly upon the window from a low angle to project
shadows of themselves so that they could be seen in
silhouette on the blind, appearing there in the form of
a Frankenstein-like figure, arms held out and fingers
stretched out as menacing claws, the face presented in
profile with the mouth wide open ready to devour its
victim. The shadows projected on the blind, momentarily diminishing the light in the room, had made Wendy
look at the window; she had screamed out as if stricken
by terror, but instantly the scream turned to a shriek, for
she recognised the trick and, in that moment, Yvonne
looked at the shadow play, too, and joined Wendy in
the shrieking laughter. The men continued their performance for two or three minutes, though they could
think of no other image than the one already projected,
merely twisting their open-clawed hands and closing
and opening their mouths wide, but each little repeated

movement on the screen was sufficient to elicit renewed shrieks of laughter from Wendy and Yvonne. Suddenly the sun fell behind a cloud, a general greyness settled on the blind, and Wendy went to open the door. The two men had assumed grave expressions as if to suggest that they had not been the cause of the recent merriment, but now Wendy was inspired to say, 'Dr Jekyll and Mr Hyde, I presume?' and her remark being received as a capital joke, everyone began laughing again. It was at that moment that Brenda had gone down and observing the tail-end of the comic drama and on being given a rapid account of the earlier sequence had burst into a long fit of laughter that was just abating when Max went down. Now he had to be told the whole story by Yvonne and Wendy. 'Suddenly there appeared this monster in the window,' Yvonne began but could not go on because she began to laugh, and Wendy took over, saying, 'With a mouth as wide as a shark's,' but now she could not proceed for the laughter and Yvonne spoke the next line, and so on, the two alternating, neither being able to complete a single idea because each was too overcome by the unbearable comedy of it all, and as they spoke and laughed, Brenda laughed, too, and Mark and Andy tried hard to pretend that, really, they did not know what the fuss was all about, but they could not keep up the studied indifference which supposedly made the joke funnier and they, too, ended up laughing with unsuppressed gusto.

'You two, honestly!' Brenda said, looking at the two men, and Max observed an unaccustomed brightness fill her eyes as she did so. 'I suppose you've earned your tea,' she added after a pause, and seeing that the merriment had ended, went off to the kitchen.

Yvonne glanced at Max, whose laughter had sounded a little forced, and catching Wendy's eye, gave a slight, almost imperceptible jerk of her head to communicate the thought that some people had no sense of humour, and Wendy signalled back her agreement with a quick flick of her eyebrows. 'We should be helping Brenda,' Yvonne said, making for the door, and Wendy, following her, exclaimed, 'I'd almost forgotten! I was going to beat the eggs for her.'

'Give them a good beating,' Mark said aloud just when they were out of the door, and Andy added, 'He knows you're good at it', whereupon Mark commented, 'One learns the hard way', and the women, who, anticipating a witty repartee, had paused outside the door, and having had their expectation fulfilled, shrieked and scurried away to the kitchen. The men smiled at each other, the brightness in their eyes conveying mutual congratulations on the success of their wit.

The door to the next room was partly open, showing a corner of a neatly made bed with a dark blue eiderdown upon it. Since it was his girlfriend Wendy's room, Mark opened the door wider, removed the hound's tooth sports jacket he was wearing, and placed it carefully on the edge of the bed. A French window opened out on the back garden where the apple tree was being buffeted by the wind. That Max had remained coldly silent when he had exchanged witticisms with Andy had irritated Mark and to see if the man had any sense of humour at all he now came up with what he believed was a manly piece of wit—'Look at that tree being tossed!'—and glanced at Max. He looked out at the tree but it was Andy who responded with, 'It's being jerked by that panting wind', whereupon both Mark and Andy laughed aloud. Andy paused to add, 'It'll soon spill its seed', before continuing to laugh. Both noticed, however, that their wit made no impression on Max and that their laughter, which the girls found so infectious, barely provoked him to smile. Aware that some response was expected from him, Max said when the two stopped laughing, 'There's a line in Lawrence—"apples falling like great drops of dew"—it just occurred to me that that's impossible, I mean has anyone ever seen *great* drops of dew, and yet it's a beautiful image, striking and memorable.'

"Quite,' said Andy, though later when he recounted the story to the girls after Max had left, he would repeat, 'striking and memorable' several times in a voice both exaggeratedly pretentious and ironical.

After his remark about the apples Max had left the men and gone up to Brenda's room and stood at the window there looking down on the apple tree. The wind had dropped and its branches were still. Little

half-grown apples had fallen on the lawn. The tree did
not produce edible fruit, he recalled from the previous
autumn when Brenda had moved into the flat, it had
been planted more for its blossoms in the spring. It deco-
rated the garden, that was all, and normally was scarcely
noticed. He decided to return to the sitting room, his
absence would be seen as rudeness; but when he was
going down the steps he saw Yvonne and Wendy come
out of the kitchen, each carrying a tray with the tea
things, and go into the sitting room from where, as
Yvonne opened the door, Andy's voice was heard to say
loudly, 'Here come the maids of honour!' Max reached
the bottom of the stairs. He made to go into the sitting room but just as he was nearly at the open door he
noticed that the group was engaged in setting the table
for tea; the girls were laughing, there was a tinkling of
cups and saucers and a clattering of plates and cutlery,
and Mark's deep voice was making some remark; Max
paused for a second, remained unnoticed, and walked
quietly to the front door, opened it gently and silently
let himself out.

Early summer evening outside, the wind as if riding
over some undulating landscape across a desolate moor,
rising and falling, the High Street shops closed but still a
jostling crowd on the pavements, buses waiting to turn
at the Church Street traffic lights, Angus Steak House
filled with diners, shiny faces seen through the window,
knives and forks among the meat and potatoes, mouths

opening and closing, hands raising glasses of red wine, everyone apparently pressed by an anxiety to appease an insatiable appetite, cars barely moving in the street, many with lonely drivers whose eyes stare out wearily, and on the wide pavement in front of Barker's the crowd is walking around a middle-aged woman in a flowery mini skirt whose two Airedales, each on a separate leash, have run around her in opposite circles and bound her legs between her ankles and knees and in her attempt to free herself she is slowly spinning around on her heels but while one leash loosens the other one tightens and she spins in one direction and then the other, alternately pulling and letting go now on one leash and now on the other, without becoming unfettered which seems to entertain the dogs who take little leaps at her.

Past Wimpy's, then past Wheeler's, opposite Kensington Palace Hotel, there's Stannie in the Goat in his red tie and blue jacket, taking it slowly with only a half pint of Watney's Red Barrel, and though you're not late he's already been there a quarter of an hour, and seeing you goes to the bar and fetches a half pint for you while you sit down and light a cigarette. 'What's it all about, then, like the taxi driver asked Bertrand Russell?' Stannie says, as usual half joking and half cynical, and you, knowing the story, say, 'And you know something, old Russell didn't have an answer, not a clue!' Stannie laughs, it's a good one, the great philosopher not having a clue, being helpless before a taxi driver's simple question, 'But how could a taxi driver have recognized Russell,' asks Stannie, 'and furthermore how could he have posed a question in philosophy?' Two tables away someone had abandoned the *Evening Standard* and you point to it and say, 'It's all those ban-the-bomb stories, Russell's been in the papers a lot.' And in fact, now that you look, the *Standard*'s been left open at a page that has a picture of Russell, and so Stannie's vision must have registered that when he rose to fetch the half-pint and somewhere in his unconsciousness he must have had the association of Russell and the taxi driver anecdote. 'Philosophy!' you say and sigh and take a sip and morosely add, 'All I see is Aristotle spanking Alexander's bottom. And the worst of it is it didn't do any good, it didn't stop Alexander from trying to conquer the world.' And Stannie says, 'Can't imagine Bertrand Russell playing the taws upon the bottom of Harold Macmillan', and tips the rest of his half-pint down his throat and you take a long swallow and rise to fetch two more halves.

Barely distinguishing Stannie and you among the interior shadows in his passing glance, Max walked past the Goat, looked down De Vere Gardens, and then, coming to a zebra crossing, decided to go into Kensington Gardens, for there was a fair and foul light and pale blue and metallic grey sky, the pull and release of English weather that persuaded him he must go walk on grass, always these contradictions within his spirit, desire and loathing, pale blue and metallic grey, the tumbling light on the summer-green grass. Brenda was of this earth, a peasant woman really, happiest baking a cake, for whom three years at the university and B. A., second class, second division, had had only one goal, the job she got at Ponting's as buyer of women's clothes, an honest homely woman really, no passion stimulated her flesh that was not domestic, her emotions remained consistently utilitarian, Bake and eat, her unexpressed motto, love a matter of making sure the oven was properly pre-heated before putting the cake-mix in. In *Geology*, of all subjects, her second class, second division B. A., a down-to-earth study of Time could one but appreciate the timeless beauty of a fossil; but the second class, second division humanity was composed of people who learned a formula by rote and never looked at the form of a thing, who could read a string of words in the best accent and never suspect it was a phrase from Shakespeare. Striding across the grass and looking up at the windy turbulence among the clouds, Max took a deep breath as if he could thus filter out the metropolitan soot and draw down into his lungs only the pure air that hung high above London. Ludicrous, that image of himself being placed in her pre-heated oven though the way the affair was going god only knew when the bloody thing would get hot enough, but that was not what had made him walk out of her flat, the realisation entered his brain with a surge of oxygen, it was the disappointment that one could live and have no concept of life, he had made a sudden, instinctive and unpremeditated exit because behind that disappointment was an enormous sadness that three years at the university had meant nothing to the great second class, second division majority, and the memory that had come to him when he quietly closed the door was of Brenda, when he first asked her out, wanting to see *South Pacific*, which, she said, she had seen twice before, it was her very favourite film. He was walking parallel to Kensington Road and stopped, seeing Napier's statue at the top of Queen's Gate, and decided to walk back and make his exit down Palace Gate, take the 49 bus there. Dark grey clouds were being dragged across the sky by the wind like huge tents that the wind had ripped from their moorings, filling the air with a dust storm of gloom, but the sky still was patched by little areas of brightness and though no shadows were cast on the ground some surfaces held on to the dull glint of a pearly sheen and preserved clearly marked definitions. It was a nice sentimentality, to admire a girl's ordinariness, a condescension, rather, to be charmed by her dullness of mind and to flatter her vulgar taste as though it were a natural simplicity infinitely to be esteemed, provided, of course, each time he smilingly endured her thoughtless drift there followed a sequel in bed, ah yes, he had only his own egotism and snobbery to blame, poor Brenda was only being herself. Coming opposite Palace Gate, Max saw people hurrying down Broad Walk and making for the exit as if anxious to escape some imminent calamity. The sky had gone a shade darker, the billowing canvas of the spreading grey clouds stretched across the little patches of brightness, there had developed a roaring turmoil in the atmosphere, a murmur of distant thunder, and the upper branches of the elms were being whipped and flung diagonally by the wind. Max stood still. The crowd hurried out of the Gardens, the windswept Broad Walk clean. Max remained there, his back to the exit, looking up at the rising paved expanse, not a soul on it where there was a strolling crowd a moment ago, and not seeing the throng among the barely moving cars and buses on Kensington Road behind him, he experienced a sense of bodily disengagement, all alone there, a receptacle of perceptions of shocking clarity. Those sunlit blossomy days, banks covered with daffodils and tulips, those late summer overcast evenings when rhododendrons empurpled the gloom, those surprisingly blue days of crystal clear light in mid-winter, the leafless branches glazed with ice, or those drizzly days of dripping mid-summer, how fragments of time from past seasons and no doubt seasons to come seemed now a hallucinatory present as the wind's low wolfish moan pursued the fleeing humans, as if the tempest that had suddenly sprung up made one's memory a repository of fantasies, foul and fair.

You come out of the Goat with Stannie, both of you with hands in coat pockets, leaning forward into the

cool wind, and walk hurriedly down De Vere Gardens.
You have posed a question—'If Bertrand Russell is at
Liverpool Street station to catch a train to Cambridge
and looking up at the clock sees it's 12.15, and if on the
same day Karl Popper is on a platform at St Pancras to
catch a train to Crewe and looking up at the clock sees it's
12.15, would the two times exist independently of each
other, and if Russell's time could have no knowledge of
Popper's time, nor Popper Russell's, would that constitute
a refutation of time?' Stannie has been thinking about it
and coming to the door of the house where you're about
to enter, stops, looks at you, and says, 'Why should
anyone, let alone a philosopher, want to go to Crewe?'

At a future date, cutting across Broad Walk towards
the corner exit near Kensington Palace Hotel, you will
look down De Vere Gardens where most of the houses
will have been converted to hotels and you will not
remember what the occasion was that brought Stannie
and you to that door, nor what was past the door, whether
someone's residence where the host was the patron of
a string quartet or some institute that held concerts of
new chamber music in the long first-floor room, and nor
will you remember what happened to Stannie once you
had entered, except that he had just said, 'Wasn't Popper
from Vienna?' Perhaps he was not a patron, the host,
but a fond father, for the cellist was a young woman
of twenty or so, his daughter, with black hair falling to
her shoulders from a precise middle parting and dark

brown eyes fixed anxiously on the score, or perhaps she was not related to the man and he was not the host but the director of some institute that promoted new music and when introducing the quartet had spoken warmly about the cellist that will have remained in your memory as a fatherly tone, but then the music was not new, for a phrase from the cello will come back to you, play with a sudden start inside your ear when cutting across the Broad Walk at a future date you will look down De Vere Gardens, and you will utter the one word, *Bartók!* and in that moment you will remember the first time you saw Jenny Byrne.

But then what happened? How is it that on another day you and Jenny are walking past the Round Pond in that slow, dilatory manner of young lovers? What was the weather then, what the season, the two of you in that absorbed manner of lovers, was it not autumn, your eyes on the ground rapt in admiration of her ankles, were there not fallen leaves from the chestnuts and the elms on the grass, were there not torn branches from the elms? Her skirt that swung into your vision with each step, red and green and black, when did your hand caress the soft wool, the tartan taut against her thigh? Was it a day, a week, a year after the concert where you saw her eyes stare in momentary amazement at the score that indicated the next bar should be played forcefully and at the same time be drawn out and then, when she had executed the intricate passage, her eyelids sank

down for a second, relieved to have overcome the difficult moment, a little satisfied glow in her eyes when
she raised the eyelids and just before returning to the
score looked at the balding violinist who nodded almost
imperceptibly his approval while himself still not finished with the passage, was it yesterday or a week or
a year later from that moment when you walked with
her past Round Pond, torn elm branches at her feet?
How could you have known what was marked on the
score, you who can't read music, so was it she who talked
about it, described and explained the musical difficulty,
but when could that have been? What transfixed you,
the music in your ears or the image in your eyes of her
bare arm as it thrust the bow in rapid short stabbings
across the strings and the simultaneous movement of
her head that shook her straight black hair and sent a
ripple across her bosom? *String Quartet No. 4 by Béla
Bartók*, said the programme in your hand, but did you
hear anything at all or did your eyes shut off your other
senses finding in the curve of her neck and the lower
calf that showed below the dark grey skirt more art than
could saturate your blood and madden its circulation
with desire? When her arm drew slowly to a pause and
she pressed her lips together seeing on the score that she
must fade the cello away into silence, a relief in her eyes
that her hands and nerves had not faltered during the
difficult passage, did the sympathetic anxiety in your
heart not also subside, but when in the next moment

she glanced quickly at the balding violinist as if seeking his approval for her execution and though he did not look at her there was still some obscure signal exchanged for you read in her expression, her lips opening slightly and the flesh at her cheeks relaxing from the stiffness of the earlier clenched-jaw concentration, a profound contentment which seemed to you clearly to imply how important it was for her to receive the balding violinist's approval, perhaps even his praise, and did your heart not become troubled with a new anxiety and your blood begin to rage with the irrational fury of a jealous lover? Why else were your ears suddenly afflicted with deafness, for though your eyes continued to see her white fingers against the cello's black neck, going up and down on the fingerboard, though you watched hypnotically her right hand almost fisted over the end of the bow as she drew it across the strings now in tense slow motion and now in a seeming fit of irrepressible rage, the moving arms of the three others in the quartet in your peripheral vision, whatever the harmony or discord sounded in the room or whatever the passion or pain or pleasure was suggested by the composition, why did you hear nothing but sat grieving instead that the balding violinist was her lover? Did you not see him as a *balding* violinist because you wished to attach a disparaging idea to his person, to reduce his potency as a lover in your projected speculation of her affair with him? Her quick smile as she caught his eye when the quartet ended, the applause in the room that awakened your ears, the second violinist, a thin man with a prominent nose, exchanging smiles with the stocky violist whose sparse beard barely covered acne scars, a warm enthusiasm in the applause expressive of that contentment which is experienced as a complete happiness that's unrelated to any social condition or ideological interpretation but is a possession of all one's senses by the abstract thing called art, why then, in all that commingling of wellbeing when all seems right with the world, did you remain oppressed, was it not perfectly natural that the cellist should smile at the first violinist? Slightly flushed her pale cheeks, shyly overwhelmed her eyes in their surprise at the continuing applause, she bowed, she curtsied, all her being confused with happiness, and you, you could not bring your hands to strike against each other, were you envious also of the hundred other pairs of eyes that looked at her and you did not wish yours to seem just one of them? Was it the vanity of incipient passion, the awful conceit of the self that demands an exclusivity of possession even when the upsurge of desire is only a fleeting hypothesis, an unexpressed and entirely arbitrary proposal to a stranger's outward form, why else should misery have depressed your spirit until you could speak to her, until she looked only at you?

She had never seen you before and, bowing for the fifth time, her cheeks suffused with happiness at the continuing applause, she did not see you, perceiving only an audience, before finally walking away to an adjoining room. But there you are, crossing the bridge over the Serpentine, stopping there to look at the Westminster skyline, a flag waving over parliament, and you have your hand on her hip just below her short grey jacket where the sun falling on her skirt's red tartan shows its true colour, scarlet, and makes vivid the green in the green and black pattern, her navy blue angora sweater behind her unbuttoned jacket like fur shining in the sunlight as after a sudden rain shower. She has her hand at your waist, pressed into the side of the jacket of your brown suit with burgundy pinstripes, and when she talks, she calls you Maxey, already using the name she has chosen for you, so you have been intimate for some time now, for you do remember that moment when, her lips close to yours, she said, 'Max is too abrupt, too harsh, you are Maxey', a lingering affectionately expressed *ee* that made your name musical when she spoke it. Still, no association takes you back to the primal moment. Accidental or deliberately contrived the beginning: if the latter, it involved strategic planning, working out directions that had to be rigorously followed, as if referring to a user's manual; or, if a spontaneous event, unpredicted and unforeseen, merely one of the billion possibilities that precede a collision, it followed a long period of unthinking subsistence, an unexpected big bang, and all at once, like the Queen of the Night suddenly appearing in the sky, there was lightning

and thunder, then glorious music, and you found yourself awakened in some magical world, enchanted by a
beautiful apparition. The sun went behind a cloud, a
shadow fell over parliament, and there was an eruption
of children's voices, a party of eight or ten year-old girls
coming up the pavement on the bridge, walking in pairs,
blue gingham frocks under navy blue cardigans, navy
blue berets on mostly blond heads, rosy cheeks and pink
mouths, a warbling and squeaking of continuous words,
a large-bosomed teacher with horn-rimmed glasses like
a shepherdess behind the little flock of girls, directing
them towards the Albert Memorial, and, 'Jenny,' you
said, 'let's go boating'.

And a quarter of an hour after you'd stood upon it
you were rowing under the bridge, and in that strange
sensation of simultaneously perceiving the before and
the after you sensed yourself observed by the former self
of fifteen minutes ago still on the bridge and yourself
perceived the self yet to exist fifteen minutes hence under
the willow branches, Jenny in your arms, who now was
steering the boat towards the farther shore on the Long
Water. You looked over your shoulder and worked the
oars to follow the direction Jenny was taking as if the
mysterious spontaneity that had brought you together
now guided the succeeding events of your relationship
and you found yourself where you had never expected
to be and though you had neither an understanding nor
any knowledge of the causes that brought you there yet

your whole being was imbued with relief and contentment that you were there, with Jenny.

On the banks of rivers and lakes, its branches arching
and leaning over the lapping water and cascading down
to the glassy surface, the ends eternally sucking there, the
loveliest of trees, the weeping willow! Its branches hang
like a curtain swaying in the slight breeze or billowing in
a wind, or, when the air is still and heavy, bend and drop
into their reflections in the polished obsidian surface of
the water, or merely fall there like a beaded screen or like
long strings of thickly knotted flowers, deep green in the
overcast gloom or scintillatingly lit by the thousand twin-
kling spots like fireflies hovering over the water when
the sun breaks through. Behind the screen of the overhanging branches, in the secluded dimly lit cave, a swan
or an egret might be nesting, perfectly still and silent,
but with a throbbing in its neck, its eyes attentive to the
slightest shimmer, as when a dragonfly stabs the water's
surface, or a bee bursts in, buzzes furiously, and is gone
in a second; or there might be a water snake wiggling
through the rushes on the edge of the bank hunting for
the eggs of mallards; or sitting on a projecting root, in
the cool den made by the willow's branches, might be a
beaver inspecting the shadows of hundreds of tadpoles
flickering in the water. Always looking, these creatures,
for some enclosed and secure space, or arriving there
without actively searching but driven there by instinct,
as if nature which gave the colour white to flowers that

open only at night had hung the willow's branches to create private enclosures and they arrived there, just as the night moth was drawn to the white flower, blindly. A person standing on the opposite bank, idly watching the rowers coming into the Long Water, his eye caught for a moment by the blue of a young woman's sweater, his attention distracted then by the little boy with him, and when he looks again, vaguely searching for the woman he had noticed sitting astern and working the rudder while her male companion rowed, and not seeing her, concludes that she must have directed the boat back to the Serpentine for she's nowhere to be seen. And another, walking down the path from Peter Pan, glancing at the farther shore and seeing the water there agitated though there's no wind, for he can see the willow's branches are dead still, but funny, he flicks his head in that shrugging gesture which admits there are some incomprehensible phenomena in this world, there's a semi-circle of bobbing waves round where the willow's branches weep into the water, like some angler had hooked a large fish and it was thrashing under the surface.

The cello between her legs, the grey skirt falling behind it in folds, held, though not pressed by, her knees, her face turned up and eyes closed as her hand glides the bow in the slow drawn out prelude to the second movement, a darkness of feeling accessed from some deep recess within the heart, a slight mournful shaking of her head that sends a wave down her black hair, the first violin pierces the air, but distantly, the pizzicato plucking of strings, then the scherzo's eruption, a sudden violent assault, her head shaking from side to side, the black hair falling across her face, nothing in the world but the crashing, shattering harmony, a collapse then, all emotion drained, a descent into near silence, a bird in a nearby bush perhaps rehearsing a little air, some little warble in the trees, but a second scherzo pierces the air briefly, as brutal as before in that rage of deepest torment within the human breast, her head shaking violently, then finally almost a resigned harmony, the sinking of the spirit in the peace of the interior self lulled in the cool shade of memory by unheard melodies.

In the archaeology of the self, in that deep dig where you discover the broken fragments with which you assemble the mosaic of memory, you form only a partial history, for some of the bits and pieces that you glue together as images of a plausible truth have an uncertain probability—take away the little jagged piece that seems to fit as an eye on a face and place it in another equal space and it fits perfectly as a knot on the bark of a tree—and what might have been the event or face that you recollect with such conviction could be only an invention or the imagination's borrowing from art, pictures at an exhibition.

Snatches of music, as if the windows were open in De Vere Gardens on a still summer's day and all else in London had fallen silent, that first scherzo again erupted in his ears and at once agitated all his other senses. Her lips so close to his they kissed lightly when she spoke, 'Maxey,' she said, '*Max!* is like a sudden burst from a trombone, but *Maxey* is like hearing a dying note on a horn in the depth of a forest, beautiful and haunting'. *Jenny Byrne, Jenny Byrne*, he repeated her name, like a child at the piano, two fingers striking the same keys again and again.

She lived with her widowed mother in a small flat in Bramham Gardens. Max saw Jenny there only once, when the mother went to North Wales for three days to visit an ailing sister. He scarcely spent an hour with Jenny in her little room with its narrow bed. Though absent, the mother seemed omnipresent in the flat's tidily arranged clutter of porcelain figures, a Wedgewood tea service, dried flowers in baskets, framed pictures of her husband in a captain's uniform, his two medals in a frame on the wall, and a cuckoo clock that made a whirring sound before it sang out each quarter of an hour. Max was told the family history—the father's death in Normandy, the mother's struggle, her devotion to her gifted daughter who won a place at the Royal College of Music—but all that was incidental to the person of Jenny and unconnected to the idea of love, a vague and elusive concept that somehow insisted that the essential experience of it remain in some pure realm, some pre-lapsarian state, uncontaminated by the presence or the thought of others. If she told him about her days at the Royal College, or how she became one of the

Brompton Quartet, and what her relationship had been with the balding violinist, Max put the information in that pile of papers which, though of some significance, one hopes not to need to consult again. She spent the mornings practicing and the afternoons rehearsing with the Quartet in a studio they rented in Cromwell Road, a time from which Max was necessarily excluded; sometimes he waited for her in a pub on Earls Court Road round the corner from the studio and the moment he saw her enter he could tell from the expression on her face that the music she had been rehearsing had drained her of emotion and turned her flowing blood to a stagnant pool or had imported to the chemistry of her brain an element of a hitherto unsuspected passion, provoking in her flesh a fever of expectation. The source of the varying mood was inevitably associated with the nature of the particular afternoon's engagement with the music being rehearsed; sometimes the difficulty of a passage left her frustrated and unhappy with herself, and the patience with which her colleagues stopped and restarted that part of the movement was like an unspoken reprimand that made her falter in the succeeding attempt and make a bad performance worse; on another day she had no problem at all with a piece even more difficult and she came away glowing with happiness, filled with the thrilling pleasure of knowing the marvellous depth of her talent. Except for some question of musical technique, Max preferred her not to explain what had happened at a rehearsal. Given four human beings, and one of them a beautiful young woman, there had to be unspoken emotional rivalries among them, the unconscious desire of one male to appear superior to another and to be seen as the most attractive mate. When Max and Jenny were together in the evening there was neither time before nor time after, no world not exclusively inhabited by their singular bodies, in space of infinite extension, and when they lay on the earth in an obscure corner behind the rhododendron bushes near the Flower Walk, all of space was contracted to that spot where he had thrown his coat and they lay upon it side by side in an embrace, that point between now and then and between here and there, the very centre of Kensington Gardens, in that eternal night.

But one evening you are in the Amphitheatre in Covent Garden, up in the gods, Massinet's Manon on the stage bringing tears to Jenny's eyes, on another evening you are together in Wigmore Hall, a quartet from eastern Europe rendering Beethoven with so solemnly reverential a concentration that Jenny leans slightly forward in her chair and listens with an amazed sort of attention, more with her eyes than her ears, on another evening there is the rambunctious but appealing sound of Kurt Weil's *Mahogany* at Sadler's Wells, London for you has become a continuing festival of music, there is Stravinsky at the Festival Hall converting the violent chaos of remembered experience to a music of such

overwhelmingly peaceful beauty—the shocking outburst
of the whole orchestra giving way to muted and grad-
ually dying bassoons followed by the measured return
of the strings before the entire orchestra erupts again
and transforms the original chaos into an unbelievable
and immortal harmony—that you sense Jenny holding
her breath, as if it was she who had been trapped in
the Infernal Dance, and then part her lips to let escape
a silent sigh, herself released by the Firebird come to
free her soul, and then there is the whole summer of
Proms at the Albert Hall, some evenings of such heavenly
splendour when you and Jenny come out hand in hand,
Vaughan Williams's lark seemingly singing among the
chestnut trees in Kensington Gardens and the sky still
palely lit by the northern sun, that you wander into the
unfenced part of the park, there is a lightness in Jenny's
step, as if she walked not on the grass but in the air above
it, her steps the choreographed pacing of a dance.

Came another autumn then and a fortnight's tour
for the Brompton Quartet of provincial cities in the
Low Countries—Maastricht, Haarlem, Antwerp, Lille.
It was the breakthrough the group had been desperate
for, hoping to win in Europe a more serious reputation
than it had in England. Naturally, Jenny was excited. It
was a small start, but a significant one. With luck, with
hard work, so much could follow. The Quartet could
now dream of a contract with Decca, of performances
in Paris, Milan, Vienna. New York even. 'Wouldn't it be

something,' she said in her excitement, 'to play Bartók in Budapest, Shostakovich in Moscow!' The Brompton Quartet would become synonymous with modern music, it would give world premieres of works by living composers. Max could see the dream in her eyes, the brown pupils seeming black with brightness. But she had to tell him who had made it possible for the Quartet to be launched in Europe, a name already known to him but almost never uttered between them. Claude Huseman.

He had been a student of composition when Jenny was at the Royal College, graduating and returning to his native Belgium in the same summer that Max had met her. There had obviously been an attachment between them. Max had seen him twice—one of the occasions a party given in a flat in Earls Court Square by some of Jenny's college friends—and while Max preferred to hear no details of his relationship with Jenny, there were enough unmistakable signs to indicate that there had been, and perhaps still was, an attachment between them, though how close it was hard to tell because when she was with Max it was as though she loved no one else. At the party, Claude had left early and she had gone out to the hall with him; it was at least ten minutes before she returned and a little later when Max was dancing with her and kissed her there was a faintly unfamiliar taste when his tongue touched the inside of her upper lip. He drew back. The suddenness with which he did so and stared at her in a moment's silent accusation, seeing in her surprised eyes a look both of alarm that he had guessed correctly and also one of defiant indifference as though it was none of his business who else she kissed, confirmed his suspicion, but he did not speak of it, still clinging to his idea of not wanting his relationship with Jenny to be marred by an association with another, and easily deluded by his own vanity to believe that she now loved him exclusively and if she had kissed the other once more it was only to put a period to that which had concluded, like kissing a dead person before the coffin is closed. But stubbornly though he held on to his delusional belief, especially after Claude had returned to Belgium, that faint unfamiliar taste would embitter his tongue on those occasions when, though her arms clasped him tightly, she remained in some inexplicable and sullen mood, and he felt as if a speck of Claude's saliva communicated to the tip of his tongue by the inside of Jenny's upper lip was continuously spreading within him like a miniscule mark that inevitably expands by some mathematical law, as of a fractal, into an unexpected and irrepressible pattern.

Lady of unspoken, obscure sorrows, lady with the beautiful face of silence, when he lay upon you beside the rhododendrons what torment palpitated within your breast that your eyes which expressed a desire exclusively for him yet dilated with apprehension that the other must be permanently banished? Why the sudden flinching, lady, though your arms held him tightly to your breast as if to eliminate all matter between the two bodies, had scorpions entered your veins and crawled into your heart, why that quick rush of the blood, the sudden hot flush, when you pressed him closer still, and almost immediately why the shiver in the flesh gone instantly cold, could you not leap away from the other's shadow? Your head tilted, the long black hair falling over your shoulder, your fingers on the instrument's neck, up and down, up and down, in that repeated rehearsal of the scherzo, your lips sucked in and pressed hard together, there seemed a maddened rage when you thrust the bow with short, sharp jabs, even your elbow piercing the empty air was agog with passion, enchambered within what dream were you screaming, lady, what jungle tribe's drumbeats pounded in your ears, that your fingers ran faster and faster up and down, up and down?

The Brompton Quartet toured the Low Countries. Jenny Byrne sent Max a postcard from Maastricht to say a small, appreciative audience had attended the all-Bartók concert. Two months later she wrote a letter from Brussels. She had married Claude Huseman.

As for love, the torment devised by desire, tongues of flame sticking out of the body, as in a medieval painting of a body in hell, he accredited with retrospective credence her expressed affirmation that there was only one who could be the object of love, *You*, and he, licked by the flames, like the body laid out on a heap of dry twigs on the riverbank for cremation, understood that love was an eliminator of identity, for it set fire to the individual flesh and sought a purity of form so absolute it was unattainable except as an abstraction felt as a dissolution of the self in that coupled climax when the *I* smashes through the mirror of fleshed reality into the *You*, shattering space into fragments and simultaneously flinging a fist at time in its longing to grasp orgasm as an eternal moment.

Heavy in the damp air the rhododendron blossoms, sweet the echo in the Gardens of unheard melodies, silence falling from the rhododendron blossoms as rolling mercury drops of moisture, *You . . . You . . . You . . .*, only *You* in this garden, in London.

Perhaps there was an unknown dimension that influenced human behaviour and imposed a choice on us contrary to our conscious predilection, some faint scent that we must follow, abandoning all present attachments and dismissing as perjury our former professions of love, perhaps it was merely a choice nature made in its ceaseless hunt for that sexual pairing which best advanced genetic selection and disguising that choice as a sentimental decision persuaded the individual that one love was *truer* than another, there was always another *You*.

The echo in the Gardens of a sequence of notes, the

bow gliding over the strings, the hand suddenly frenzied and then calmly caressing the neck, her eyes opening, listening in that long summer twilight as if sound were silent but visibly fell from the rhododendron blossoms, frenzied again, unrestrained and climactic, empurpled the red blossoms in that light, the night throbbing in the garden, in London.

So that even when in an absent friend's borrowed flat in Edith Grove, one whole night three days before she crossed the Channel, Jenny lay with her head on Max's chest, her lips so close to his heart it did not beat but inhaled and exhaled her breath, when they lay together in that delicious lassitude when the cooled body slowly recuperates heat—and how quickly again it was as if the body wore a shirt of flame and that word again, *love*, as if the air murmured it, the night spoke it, the cube of space in that one night heard it—even then, accepting him fully, her blood had already determined to reject him, though there was no smell in the room but of their two bodies the faint scent of the other hung outside the window and when they parted in the morning she would follow it until she bore Claude Huseman a son.

Smoke thick in the Duke of Clarence, waves of talk and laughter, noise swelling and dipping in the pervasive pubsmell, mostly of beer, and Stannie is in the middle of one of his philosopher's puzzles . . . 'and if Plato's ghost appeared would it be real or only a form' . . . and while Max listens and interpolates the comment, 'Assuming of course Yeats is not at some bloody séance', his eyes have been gazing at the compressed curvature created by her body's weight on the buttocks pressed down upon the red stool of a young woman leaning forward with her elbows on the bar, a glass of gin and tonic in one hand, her dark-haired head turned listening to her companion on her right so that when he looks at it Max sees her face in a shadowed profile, but he stares at the fleshy bulge beneath the dark green wool of her short skirt stretched taut at mid-thigh, finding all the woman's sexuality compressed there, and then his eyes follow the exposed left knee visible from where he sits to the calf and ankle encircled by the strap of a green square-toed suede shoe with an inch-high dark brown heel resting on the chrome ring at the bottom of the stool. The angle of her leg has tightened the flesh of her calf and given a sharp edge to its curving outline, and Max, momentarily seeing only that outline, as if it were a charcoal line on Arches paper, dismisses the possibility of a mathematical formula that could create an equation between the extent of a curve and the definitive presence or absence in it of beauty, but, of course, should the curve deviate a millimetre either way this lovely gorgeously smooth line would be as the leper's skin. 'Can a ghost be anything but form?' he responds to Stannie. 'There's Marcellus with his question, *tell me he that knows*, addressing the visiting scholar, *Who is't that can inform me?* And the foolish scholar thinks he can!' And when she leans away from the bar, accepting a cigarette from her companion, Max sees her straighten and arch her back, putting her right hand under the hair falling at her neck and giving it a quick shake before bringing the hand down to where he holds open a golden packet of Benson & Hedges and plucks one of the two cigarettes protruding from the open flip-top and in that moment the curve of her bosom within the pale green ribbed polo-neck sweater projects out as she takes in a deep breath before quickly lowering her head to reach the light the man holds up for her, and though after lighting the cigarette she relaxes and leans an elbow again on the bar, Max continues to see the rounded outline of her bosom, a thick brushline on canvas of an odalisque's voluptuous form. 'I was a scholar once,' Stannie says with a sly look in his eyes, the same when he's about to tell a joke, and therefore Max anticipates him by saying, 'And foolish you were consequently', and Stannie's eyelids drop and rise in slow motion and there's a different look, weary almost, in his eyes, so it's not a joke, and says, 'I wouldn't say foolish, reckless would be closer, yes, reckless, or intrepid, or just plain daft, for how else can you take new ideas seriously?' Max nods his head, takes a sip of his beer, glances quickly at the woman's hand at the bar, a wisp of smoke rising from the cigarette held between two finger tips, and looks at Stannie, who says, 'Until one day I couldn't get that line out of my head, you know the one, *What then, sang Plato's ghost, What then?* Let it remain a mystery, no one can bloody tell, be content with the shape of things, flowers in a garden, if you're lucky.' Suddenly, the woman comes off the stool, crushing the cigarette in an ashtray on the bar with one hand and tugging at her green wool mini-skirt with the other, and walks out with her companion, a little shiver of her buttockflesh behind the slightly creased green wool as she strides to the door, Stannie looks at his watch. There's time for another half before he walks down Drayton Gardens to see an Antonioni film at the small intimate cinema there that not long ago was a small intimate theatre for amateur productions of small intimate drawing room comedies. 'What becomes of ideas, then?' Max asks, imagining large blooming red and yellow flowers on the pale green skirt, and himself aware of the time, another forty minutes before he must go stand near the flower vendor outside Gloucester Road tube station and wait for Mirabel. Stannie goes up to the bar to fetch the beer. She was dressed for tennis, the last time Max saw Mirabel, back at the university the year he graduated, a racket pressed against her bosom, long slender legs, auburn hair parted at the centre and tied in two little pigtails that swung above her shoulders as she walked towards the courts. Stannie returns, holding the two half-pint glasses by their handles in a firm one-handed clasp. '*Love*, said Claudius . . .' says Stannie, placing the glasses on the table and then taking one up

while he sits down and quickly saying, 'Cheers!', before
going on, '. . . seeing into his nephew's soul, *his affections
do not that way tend*. What was that, then? Perception,
insight, intuition, lucky guess, scientific conclusion
based on evidence?' Max picks up his glass and says,
'Cheers', just when his lips reach the rim and after taking a swallow, adds, 'I get your idea', and Stannie, giving
a little ironical laugh, says, 'An older man and his young
mistress sail to an island . . . ,' 'A high-powered execu-
tive, 42,' Max interpolates, 'who expertly navigates his
own yacht named *Celeste* after his wife who's been left
alone in the villa on the mainland', 'Dark-haired and
dark-eyed, Monica, the young mistress, 23,' continues
Stannie, 'dark her complexion under the Mediterranean
sun, olive-coloured bare arms and legs in short-sleeved
black-and-white striped shirt, with its tail-ends tied in
a rabbit-eared knot at the navel, and navy blue shorts,
while the man's thick wavy hair is too perfectly black
and the belt of his white slacks looks a little uncomfort-
ably tight.' It's a rocky, apparently uninhabited island,
no grassy hillside on it, only scattered boulders and some
stubbly bushes as if nibbled to the ground by goats, and
the entire coast walled by rocky cliffs or blocked by
boulders, so they must drop anchor in the deep distance
and make for the dangerous shore in the small boat.
Help me, Guido! Monica calls, reaching up a hand to her
crouching lover who, attempting to exhibit youthful
virility, has already quickly clambered up the slope of a

massive rock and now turns to help his mistress who has
noticed, what he in his eagerness to be ostentatiously
virile has not, that just to their right behind some low
bushes is some old goatherd's trail that would make passage up the hill not at all problematical but has judged
that it would flatter Guido if she gave him the impression
of being helpless in this wild and inhospitable world
unless she depended on his masculine strength. Once he
has pulled her up, she rests her cheek on his shoulder and
looks up the hill. She can just see the trail winding up
towards the right with a widening fork diverging more
horizontally to the left. Guido is trying to breathe noise-
lessly through an open mouth in order to suppress the
suggestion that the physical exertion of helping her
climb up the rock has made him out of breath and hears
her say, *Look, Guido, there are two paths there*, and when
he turns, adds, *you take one and I'll take the other*, a proposal that makes him joke, *What, you want a separation
already?* to which she answers, *No, my darling, you will
see that fate intends us to join up, the two paths will meet*,
and before he can make a choice she springs away and
bounds up the wider and less steep path on the left. He
watches her a minute, his eyes bright with self-congrat-
ulation in that moment's estimation of what he pos-
sesses, and stares with proprietary gratification at her
fluid body that in its dance-like flight leaves an impression of musical notes against the hillside. But he's put
to the test now, having the steeper path to negotiate, and

is obliged to nourish with preliminary athletic steps the
illusory root of youthfulness and heaves himself up with
long, fluid strides. If the two paths meet at the top, his
has to be the shorter passage, and therefore he can per-
mit himself a little rest after each strenuous upward
thrust. The third time he stops, he's surprised, on turning and looking at the ocean, how high he already is and
how far out in the sea the *Celeste* is anchored: a confusion of measurements has arisen in his mind creating an
inexplicable suspicion about direction and his eyes, narrowing as he looks at the *Celeste* in the manner of one
bothered by the glare, remain screwed up when he
resumes his climb until he remembers the pair of dark
glasses placed earlier in his shirt pocket. Though the path
Monica has taken is less conspicuous as a passage to the
top of the hill, it is obvious, from the profusion of scattered droppings upon it, that it is the one over which
the goats have been driven, perhaps as recently as the
previous evening, and when she turns round the curve
of the hill, from where she can no longer see the *Celeste*,
she observes that her path leads to a flatter area at the
end of which is a stone ruin, as if there was once a cot-
tage there that has long been neglected. Then she begins
to hear the bells, a little faint tinkling at first and then a
continual jumbled and inharmonious ringing. She was
mistaken, it's not a stone ruin but an improvised shelter,
small and large rocks piled any which way provided they
can form four walls, with a fisherman's net thrown over

the top filled with dried torn-up shrubs for a roof. Past
the shelter, in a pen on sloping ground, ten or a dozen
goats become visible, all but three of them lying on the
ground, and it has been from the bells at the throats of
these three who have been running around the pen in
some goatish game of predatory lust and rejection that
Monica has been hearing the discordant ringing. She
proceeds along the path and on coming to the front of
the shelter notices that a gap has been left on its front
wall to make a door. She does not stop until she has
walked some seven or eight steps beyond the shelter and
then, thinking that she'd seen something curious when
going past the door, something that caught and reflected
the light, she walks back and stops in front of the door.
One of the goats bleats just then, another answers.
Sunlight seeping through the gaps among the shrubs on
the net comprising the shelter's roof is falling on a man's
dark and wrinkled face and shining back from his eyes.
He's seated on the ground. Long and straggly his curly
black hair, the dark and wrinkled skin must be the result
of long days in the sun, there's a muscular firmness in
his torso, his body is younger than his face. His hand
jerks up quickly, a gesture telling someone to *stop, don't
move, don't speak*, and Monica notices that there's a
young boy of thirteen or fourteen, bare-chested and
bare-legged, next to him who was perhaps about to
move or speak. She looks at the boy, then stares at the
man, two statues now, fixed and silent as the rocks on

the island, their stony eyes watching her. The goats commence a chorus, quickly abandon it, only the bells ringing from the throats of the three still at their lusty game.
She glances again at the boy and then again at the man
whose mouth now hangs open though she saw no movement, he must have suddenly opened it in the moment
she looked at the boy, a gleam of saliva-dribble at the
corners of the man's mouth, longer the silvery thread at
the left corner, extending itself in a sunbeam like the
thread of a spider's web. *Hello*, she says, but is not sure
if the word has come out of her mouth and if it has it
has been in a strange tone, not spoken as greeting, not
an expression of surprise, uttered with no expectation
of an answer, and in a confused moment, when she's not
sure whether she is where she is, she thinks that perhaps
she had spoken no word at all, only felt a sharp sting of
sunlight at the back of her neck as if a spot of light suddenly smacked her there through a magnifying lens.
'Meanwhile, Guido . . .' Stannie says and Max, staring
vaguely at the unoccupied stool and seeing still suspended there as an after-image the compressed buttockflesh in the green skirt, nods meditatively, and when he
looks again at Stannie he sees his lips talking about some
horned beast and coming to a rhetorical conclusion: 'If
you must end up in a cave with your torn-up self, where's
the adventure of love, then?' Now Max stares at Stannie
with a slightly startled look, as if there were some personal context for the remark, and discovers a picture

projected in his imagination of Claude Huseman's face transformed to the head of a satyr, a horned, narrow bony face, the mouth twisted in a leer, saliva dripping from a corner. 'Not torn up,' he says to Stannie, 'but fragmented, scattered jigsaw-puzzle pieces of a shattered mirror where the self last glimpsed itself whole.' Very deliberate and measured had been her movements, Jenny Byrne, now only an idea of what had been or what might have been, and perhaps his knowledge of her as a musician, one who obsessively rehearsed what she must perform, prompted a retrospective persuasion that she had moved slowly, deliberately, when perhaps there had been a frolicsome air to her gait, at least occasionally; what's sad is not that there's no recollection that's not contaminated by some unconnected conviction but that so soon, what, only a fortnight, the figure that was so fully illuminated its flesh sparkled and radiated a blushing glow but in the next minute, so soon, so soon, it's a silhouette, the head turning away, the whole figure a silhouette, sharply focused for a second, then disintegrating at the edges and blurring as through a rotating lens's changing focal length, and then, ha then, look how the light, or is it darkness, thumps down, and what's left in the eye that stubbornly refuses not to see but the fabrication of memory, very deliberate and measured. Mirabel in tennis clothes, instantly sportier and lighter, though of course she's not going to come to Gloucester Road dressed for tennis, but that last image of her, the strings of her racquet crisscrossing against her bosom, the pressure forming an indentation there, gave the heart a fillip, for love re-sculpts its idols and revises the idiom of its hymns, distributing stresses in new springing rhythms. Alive, in his memory then, Jenny Byrne, her eyes only on him, as his whole body pressed on her, that one night in Edith Grove, one-way street, Edith Grove, the traffic, lorries and taxis and cars, coming up from Cheyne Walk, from Battersea Bridge, London's night drivers coming from the riverbank, the rumble and the gear-grinding of the traffic below the window, and yet, surely she knew, nothing else existed, for what is it to be pressed down so utterly by the lover's body than to have the intuition spring in one's brain that the condition of love is precisely this, to know no other time, and she, her whole body straining against his, his eyes only on her, surely, surely, she must have been so wounded by the knowledge of love as to bear the scar forever by the revelation that love was both a vague fancy of the vain self, and therefore a transitory whim, and an insight into that texture of reality that eliminated from time any distinction between an instant and eternity. 'The ecstasy and the horror of the now,' Max says, 'the moment forever present though long past.' Stannie looks away from Max and says into his nearly empty half-pint, 'You can make it into a metaphysical thesis if it helps to overcome the pain.' Max observes to himself that Stannie can never be objective when they talk about women: for Stannie, a woman who leaves you betrays you. 'But it's no good, mate,' Stannie resumes after a pause, 'if physically she's gone, you can say good-bye both to the instant and to eternity, she's getting it from another man and that's the *now* that's real.' And she can so calmly forget. How could she on a summer's night slip into the garden and lie beside the rhododendron blossoms where even the traffic fumes from Kensington Road have the delicacy to curl away from the lovers' pocket of privacy and not pollute the garden's perfume, and she not have the skin over her entire body dyed by that night's deep violet, but instead, putting on her coat, crossing over to the Low Countries, there should remain nothing purplish or even a blushing pink on her skin when Claude Huseman wriggles over it with his flickering tongue, time past for her become nothing but the withdrawing tide that sucks away the shoreline debris, the froth and spume of memory. 'Then go proclaim that that extended *now* of togetherness was nothing,' Max says, 'that *kissing with inside lip*, as Leontes raged, nothing,' and he whispers to the rim of his half-pint glass, *nothing, nothing, nothing*, whereupon Stannie says, 'If you must quote the Bard, what about *Look here upon this picture, and on this*, isn't that little burr vanity what it all comes down to in the end? Grace sits upon your brow, etc., you are choice grazing land, whereas he, *mildewed ear*, etc., is but a barren moor, and yet she, stupid goat, goes joyously bleating among the thorns.' But that, speculates Stannie, implies that one's own aesthetic perception has an absolute correctness while biased cataracts becloud the vision of others, which conviction, of course, is vanity's primal belief upon which all its conclusions rest. The *now* that you want to believe in as a moment of everlasting beauty, concludes Stannie, all that lyrical effusion about the rhododendron bushes and their bloody blossoms, was perhaps for her a boring ordeal and what really thrilled her was to be taken to and taken in some sordid hotel in the Low Countries—for some the smell of semen-soiled sheets is more exciting than roses, forget about the rhododendrons. 'Have you not seen in the National Gallery a man walk right past Velázquez's *Rokeby Venus*, giving her a casual and indifferent glance, and then stand a whole quarter of an hour in front of Van Dyck's *Equestrian Portrait of Charles I* lost in total rapture at the anatomy of the horse?' The eye of the beholder, no doubt, but can anyone be a male of the human species and not be thrilled by the curve of the lady's hip, not feel that delicious fleshy weight in his hand of her left buttock, you'd think such male indifference would be impossible, the beauty is so sensational, but the fact is there are men whose greater ecstasy it is to stare not at a naked woman but at a horse's rump. 'A quick half,' Max says, standing up, and Stannie, looking at his watch and nodding, says, 'I'll have to walk fast down Drayton Gardens', and when Max returns with the beer, Stannie takes his half before Max can put it down on the table, says, 'Cheers', takes

a long swallow, mutters, 'Aaah!', places the glass on the
table and says, 'I'll probably have to run to the loo in the
middle of the film.' Seeing that he himself has no need
to hurry, Max almost whispers, 'Cheers', takes a sip, and
looking at Stannie observes a morose expression has
dropped its shadow across his face. Nothing like sitting
drinking with a man to remind one of one's sorrows with
women, and Max decides to say nothing, knowing that
Stannie hates to talk about Millie who abandoned him
for an older man in a wheel-chair, let go his athletic
squash-playing body in preference for one crippled in his
bones almost as if she needed to do penance for having
enjoyed physical love with Stannie, and such love one
whole summer, triple encores on those rosy June nights,
pleasure she'd never known before, but suddenly some
cold guilt chilled her blood and the need, like thorns
sticking into her flesh pricking her all over, for repen-
tance, and she left her Mellors, as if tending to the older
man in the wheel-chair, helping him to undress and
bathe, and each night lifting him into the chaste bed was
an act of self-charity, a form of taking the veil. Not
wanting to tell Stannie that he knew the thought that
made him morose just then and seeing him take another
long swallow in preparation for leaving for the intimate
little cinema in Drayton Gardens, Max asks, 'What happened to drawing-room comedies?' Stannie tips his glass
and pours all the remaining beer into his mouth, swallows, the morose shadow lifts from his face as, his eyes

suddenly bright, he says, 'To rejoyce for a moment, drawing-room comedies put on a double-brechted suit and
went to the barber's and got beweskered.' Alas for Guido,
though, dehydrated and dishevelled, staggering about
the island, shouting *Monica, Monica!*, until parched and
sunburned he must come to the goatherd's shelter. The
sun will be low on the horizon. The goats will have gone
silent. There will be no sound from the shelter but as
Guido slowly stumbles towards it the low sun will catch
a sudden movement in the interior—the boy springing
up from the ground and the older man simultaneously
holding up a hand to signal to the boy to remain quiet,
though what Guido will see will be only the shifting of
shadows. He will stumble three steps closer and then
stop, stand erect; he will stare at what he notices on the
ground just inside the entrance—the low sun casting its
light across the opening on a garment thrown there, a
black-and-white striped shirt.

Stands Max beside the flower vendor on the pavement
outside Gloucester Road tube station. Marguerites, dai-
sies, tulips, roses, bunches of little magenta flowers with
tiny leaves on brown stems. Clusters of people from the
lift up from the Piccadilly Line glance to the left and to
the right when they emerge from the exit, some in the
hurried gait of routine-accustomed commuters come
out and proceed without looking, among them sooner
or later must come Mirabel walking out of the darkness,

squinting a little before the red and yellow tulips catch
her eye. Schoolboys in navy blue blazers leap out of a 49
bus and go running into the station, *ting-ting* sounds
the bell inside the bus and the bus grinds up Gloucester
Road and halts at the red lights where there's a continuous blur of cars and lorries going in each direction on
Cromwell Road. There's a tall auburn-haired woman in
the group just come up the lift and hurrying out the exit
and Max imagines the long slender legs are Mirabel's and
when the group disperses, he starts to move towards her,
convinced for a second that it is Mirabel's face he sees,
but stops, realizes it was only an illusion prompted by
desire, the face is not youthful, not Mirabel's, etched by
sourness the not-youthful face, and who knows what
accumulation of disappointments knots the muscles in
her shoulders and makes her stoop as she walks away,
probably to a lonely bedsitter, he imagines, noticing her
ankles showing above the low-heeled red patent-leather
shoes are pink and swollen as if all the sorrows in her
blood had pooled there, and he continues to watch the
sad melodrama of her life he sees projected on her back
that's slowly receding in the pavement crowd when he
hears a voice say, 'So, you prefer older women?' Mirabel
is standing in front of him, smiling ambiguously, her
tone both teasing and accusatory, her head raised a little
in the spontaneous hauteur of one aware of her own
beauty, a supercilious mockery in her eyes which she
turns with a disdainful air towards the woman's receding

back before looking again at Max, so that he is first confused, then humbled, and then, when she abandons the
theatrical affectation of youthful superiority and a smile
bringing dimples to her white fleshy cheeks restores nor-
malcy to his idea of her face, recognizes the girl he's been
waiting for and cries out, 'Mirabel!', stepping towards
her. 'No,' his lips utter a moment before they press
against her cheek, 'there was something touchingly sad
about her that caught my pitying gaze.' He kisses her
cheek and draws back his face to look into her eyes.
Brightly grey-blue and sharply passionate in their
assumption of controlled possession of what they looked
at, her eyes, as if, did she but desire it, they could extract
the soul from his body. 'As for preference . . .' he says and
kisses her on her lips. 'You're always making up stories
about people,' she says, taking his arm, when they begin
to walk up Gloucester Road. But when they have crossed
Cromwell Road it is she who has a story to tell. Some
German girl named Heidi she'd met on the Channel
crossing a year ago who'd married into English aristoc-
racy. 'There are language schools in Oxford and
Cambridge where European girls go to learn English,'
Mirabel says. Poor families save desperately to send a
pretty daughter to learn English in these commercial
schools. The idea is to pay whatever it costs to be where
some of the most eligible young men in the world will
notice you. 'It's true!' Mirabel says seeing Max look a
little dubious. The man whose eye you catch might be a

future prime minister or Nobel scientist or the son of an
English earl. 'Look at Heidi, barely a year since she came
off the boat from Hook of Holland, hasn't yet crammed
enough English vocabulary into her beautiful head and
she's no longer Heidi but Lady Hornsby, mistress of
Hornsby House with its own park in the middle of
Derbyshire.' They walk past Emperor's Gate, Maurice
vaguely appears in Max's imagination like a film extra
in the incidental background framing the principal char-
acters, and he says to Mirabel, 'Is that a condition to be
envied?' She catches the remote hint of sarcasm in his
voice. O but it was not a question of a poor girl hawking
herself in the marriage market! Max loves the warmth
and bounce in Mirabel's voice when she has an idea to
defend and he throws glances at her as she talks, watching her lips. She'd seen, she says, too many girls go to
the trouble of getting a degree only to end up in a medi-
ocre marriage with a smug sort of satisfaction as if that
had been their real goal. 'Well, if that's what one really
wants,' she adds, 'why go to the pretence of learning in
Hull or Keele when a £12-a-week language school in
Oxford can get you a good catch?' They come to the
coffee bar next to Karnac Books and go in for a cappuc-
cino. Max notices a logical inconsistency in the succession of her ideas but like one who enjoys listening to a
symphony without attending to its compositional design
he remains engaged only with the music of her voice,
repeating an occasional phrase of hers as if it were a

melodic theme, thereby giving her the impression that he not only follows her idea precisely but also agrees with it, knowing that to be sufficient encouragement for her to jump from one idea to the next that leaves him to savour the continuous pleasure of hearing the bouncy rhythm of her voice. No, she has no interest in becoming a Lady Hornsby, Max is surprised to hear her say, but then realizes that though Mirabel has long completed telling Heidi's story and in a succession of associations has just been telling an anecdote about a lecturer's wife at her college who's been having an affair with an undergraduate in Mirabel's geography seminar, the phrase about having no interest in becoming a Lady Hornsby has been repeated like a refrain or a sort of inevitable punch line at the conclusion of each story. For a moment, Max wonders what not wanting to become a Lady Hornsby has to do with the lecturer's wife who drives about the East Anglian countryside in her Triumph TR2 with Eric from the geography seminar—With Eric, can you believe it, he hears Mirabel say dramatically, with Eric who thinks Mozambique is in South America, he's such an idiot, but then the lecturer's wife is not interested in his brain, is she—but the anecdote becomes mere bouncy sound in Max's hearing until Mirabel arrives at her punch line about Lady Hornsby, and he concludes that Mirabel's anecdotes have all been illustrative of a woman's assertion of her intellectual independence. He smiles and nods, and Mirabel, elated to notice that she has convinced him, begins to narrate another anecdote, but Max only hears the name of the protagonist, Priscilla, for he's reflecting on the irony that while he appears to Mirabel to be agreeing with her, his own obsession is not with her intellect but with his own growing desire to close her lips with his own, and, coming to the zebra crossing at the top of Palace Gate, he looks across at the trees in Kensington Gardens and anticipates finding a secluded spot where he can stop Mirabel's mouth with a kiss; and in that nice male hypocrisy that instinctively flatters a female mind for which at best a man has merely a condescending tolerance, Max demonstrates to her his total absorption in her story which has only his partial interest by lowering his head to place his ear closer to her mouth as they cross into the Gardens and, Mirabel's voice bouncing louder in the noise of the traffic about them, hears that Priscilla is a Catholic—A devout one, too, she's saying, but mentally she's like a rock—but since Max has not heard all the details he's unsure, as they come into the Broad Walk, why Priscilla's refusal to take the pill is evidence of her mental strength and is even more confused when Mirabel concludes her story— With her lovers she would not go against her Church by taking the pill but when she got pregnant no priest could stop her from getting an abortion—but nevertheless he smiles and nods his head, though slightly puzzled that this time Lady Hornsby does not step out to take a curtain call. He looks at Mirabel's lips that are briefly

closed and is enchanted by the rosy sheen on the full
lower one and is reminded how when they had kissed the
first time he had drawn his face back to look at hers in
wonder, being filled with joy that the beauty he beheld
permitted him such a gift, and seeing a joyful glitter in
her grey-blue eyes that looked back at him, observing
there her delight in being loved by him, he drew his face
close to hers and softly touched her lower lip with the
tip of his tongue and was thrilled to hear a little sound
of startled pleasure in her throat before she pressed her
head forward and met his tongue with hers, mutually
ardent then their exhilaration with each other; taking her
hand, he directs her towards the Flower Walk, her silent
voice now a lovely melody in his mind, and he wonders
whether they could not unobserved slip behind the rhododendron bushes but before they can reach the entrance
to the Flower Walk she stops and sneezes and taking her
hand away from his holds it in front of her mouth and
sneezes again. It's hay-fever, she says, and he sees her eyes
have suddenly acquired a redness and a ruddy tinge has
replaced the pale pink of her nose, there's something in
the air, she says, it's impossible—her voice trails off as she
sneezes again and turns round to walk quickly towards
the exit, leaving him standing for a moment in his surprise and frustration. He moves to catch up with her,
glancing back in the direction of the rhododendron
bushes and wondering if had he taken Mirabel there to
the secluded spot where he had lain with Jenny Byrne

barely two months earlier on that now magical summer night whether it would have been a form of desecration of her memory but then—ha! what memory?—what did Jenny deserve, having insulted his vanity by abandoning him so shockingly casually, on the contrary, it would have been not desecration but a perfectly gratifying form of reciprocating her insult, and catching up with Mirabel, he regrets he has lost the opportunity, how perfectly gratifying it would have been to be rubbing out whatever trace remained in that earth of Jenny by pressing Mirabel's body upon it. But walking out of the Gardens and finding Mirabel clasp his hand, his mind transmits a spiritual apology to Jenny, it was unlike him to be rude to her in absentia, and he banishes from his emotions any impulse that lingered there to injure her memory and decides that the mould of her body pressed into the earth beside the rhododendron bushes at the spot known only to him would remain her exclusive ground, and just as there were shrines devoted to particular saints and a pilgrim coming to the shrine of Our Lady of Guadalupe would not dream of addressing his prayers to Our Lady of Fatima, so there were in the parks and heaths of London little sacred plots, each the shrine of a woman he had loved, that he resolves, walking towards the High Street with Mirabel, will remain exclusively hers. The usual bottleneck in High St. Ken., the air nothing but diesel and petrol fumes. His eyes burn, nausea in his throat. Mirabel, however, seems suddenly cured of her hay-fever and is gaily talking away. Little sacred plots. Grace in Parliament Hill Fields. Brenda in Gunnersbury. Jenny in Kensington Gardens. Mirabel is talking about a fellow undergraduate named Leo and saying something about 'his game' but Max has been visualizing another of his sacred plots, under a plane tree next to a bed of tulips in St James's Park, and is perplexed about the game Leo is playing though the smile on his face shows Mirabel his complete appreciation of her story; when Mirabel looks at him in expectation of a response to what she has just said, he hazards a guess, 'Leo's having a crush on you', and her quick answer, 'That's what I think, too', relieves his anxiety that he might have guessed wrong, and when she adds, 'Why else does he never serve an ace against me?', Max realizes that the game she has been talking about is tennis. While his mind has been wandering from one London park to another, seeing ponds and weeping willows and secluded hollows surrounded by hawthorn bushes, Mirabel's words have been flowing into his consciousness and her remark about Leo not serving an ace springs open the compartment where her words have recently been stored so that what he had heard but not listened to is suddenly released in a rush of retrospective hearing. Leo is a good tennis player, quite a champion at the university, but each time he plays with Mirabel his backhand produces nothing but unforced errors and his faculty for serving aces deserts him completely. He loses to her each time.

But Max knows better than to state his conviction that Leo's game is the obvious one, lose in the field in order to win in bed, weaken the lady with flattery till she falls helpless on her back; better to let Mirabel believe that she wins because her own game is superior, for human vanity loathes condescension; and being himself a master of the subtle hypocrisy that's a natural instinct in a male who has designs on a female, Max says, 'Some of your shots are unplayable,' and lest that sound too vague, adds, 'That forehand down the line is a winner each time', a remark that produces in her mind a fantasy image of her own game that coincides with her idea of the perfect shot she often dreams of achieving and in that momentary coincidence creates in her the belief that she must already possess a full command over such perfection, and therefore, smiling in the glow of that flattering thought, is convinced that Max has a terrific eye for tennis. The traffic is stalled in the mouth of High St. Ken., and Mirabel tugs at Max's hand and begins to cross the road, walking through the black diesel smoke coming out of a taxi's tail-pipe and the heat exuded from the front of a bus, a 49 to Clapham Junction, Max notices, a foot behind the taxi; in the traffic going west, they squeeze between the rear of a Green Line coach and the sloping bonnet of a white Jaguar 3.8, and coming out to the pavement in front of Wimpy's Max looks up at the coach, it's the Green Line 717 to Woking, and hears Mirabel say, 'Come, my turn to buy the coffee',

an invitation that he interprets as an instant reward for
his praise of her tennis. Once they are in Wimpy's,
Mirabel decides to eat a hamburger while Max, fingering
the coins in his pocket, declares he's not hungry. When
she is considering which hamburger to order, he says, 'I
never know why people go to places like Woking and
Chertsey in a Green Line coach when it's so much faster
on a train. Just look at those people,' he points out the
window to the coach, 'sitting stuck in the traffic, but I
suppose it's cheaper than the train.' Having ordered her
hamburger, Mirabel says, 'Sooner or later, he's bound to
beat me', a remark that mystifies him until he realizes
she's still thinking of her game with Leo. Ah well, it's
bound to happen, his experience of such games informs
him, Leo's going to get into her bed and it will be forehand rallies all the way, just wait for the Christmas term
to begin and she goes back to the university. He watches
her lift the top bun of her hamburger and squeeze a
generous layer of ketchup on the meat. Recalling his
own last year at the university, he remembers that while
most girls were content to pair themselves with anony-
mous partners Mirabel was attracted to men who for
some reason, academic or sporting, constituted the conspicuous undergraduate elite, forming attachments with
whom made her one of the distinguished circle and provoked the envy of the other girls. She takes a large bite
of her hamburger and when she closes her mouth
ketchup oozes out at the corners of her mouth;

proceeding to chew rapidly, she says something but Max
hears only the words *you* and *missing* because her tongue
is concerned just then more with meat and crushed
onions and the mush of the soft bun than it is with language, but he imagines she's saying, *You don't know what
you're missing*, while her mouth is full of the very thing
he's missing. Her ketchup-bloodied chin and her child-
like delight in the hamburger strike him as charming
though at the same time it occurs to him that what
appears as innocence and charm in a beautiful young
woman is likely to develop into coarse vulgarity when
she's older, and sipping his coffee he looks out the window and sees a burgundy-coloured Bentley Continental
in the stalled traffic, its one passenger a balding man with
grey mutton-chop whiskers and a black moustache who
has let his hands drop from the steering wheel and is
yawning with his head thrown back. Mirabel smiles
when Max turns and looks at her. She seems happiest
when she eats. Her teeth are tinged red. She takes another
large bite and having said nothing when her mouth was
empty again starts to speak when her mouth is full.
Though he can distinguish the odd word and easily make
the connections necessary to comprehend what she's saying, he listens without hearing but merely keeps his
smiling gaze on her glittering grey-blue eyes, more
brightly blue and darkly grey in the Wimpy-lit glare, her
cheeks a-bulge and lips ketchup-red in his peripheral
vision, and in his own mouth there's suddenly the taste

of the first time he kissed her, a memory of her accepting his invitation to the little flat he shared with a rugby player in his final year at the university when instead of going to the cafeteria for dinner he offered to make her an omelette; it had delighted him to see with what eager relish she ate as if the chopped onion and salt and pepper in the two beaten eggs turned into a runny heap in hot butter had been a gourmet dish, and when, rising from the table, she had taken his hand and he'd leaned his head to touch her cheeks with his lips, she'd spontaneously turned her face and offered him her glistening lips that seemed freshly lip-glossed with butter, and in a moment his tongue was tasting again what he had eaten a few minutes earlier, onions and salt and runny eggs, except that the taste now possessed an additional dimension, one that was savagely earthy as if they were two barbarians for whom experience was not something to be savoured but to be attacked brutishly and grabbed. That eating followed by the savage oral exploration became the pattern of the six or seven times they met before he graduated and came down from the university. And that was all. Just one of the passing flirtations that include no serious intimacy, a diversion of kisses, no more. Indeed, Max had quite forgotten her during his affair with Jenny Byrne, and it was only the coincidence of Mirabel getting in touch when Jenny had gone on her tour of the Low Countries that he saw her again.

But it will not be till the autumn, on a blustery evening, brown and yellow and copper-coloured leaves running spontaneous little races on the pavements, the stripped upper branches of the plane trees thrashing wildly, sudden cold gusts springing up round corners and gripping pedestrians by the throat, people hurrying away to pubs and homes, fleeing from the nasty-weather night fast descending, that you, walking up Baker Street with Mirabel, will feel bucked up by the bleak and dreary light, your blood will be agitated by the sharp cold gusts, her arm in yours, and though the Shetland wool of her cardigan and the tweed of her coat will be covering her arm and the lined trench-coat will have padded yours, still her flesh and yours will be engrossed in deep chemical communication, a whole system of signs and equations based on a prehistoric formula will be making a myriad of calculations, this plus this equals that, divisions and subtractions, the bracketing of elements, all that knowledge known to the little bubbles of blood, yours and hers, that will have begun to bump and jostle against each other already through the layers of wool and tweed; while the fleeing pedestrians will be leaning head-down against the wind in their dash to some shelter, you two will stride head-in-air as though at some festive parade marching in jolly companionship, you will be thinking of nothing, saying nothing, making no decisions, following no directions, but your feet will be striding tumpety-tum knowing exactly where they must take you, quickly out of Baker Street and into the Outer Circle, whoosh-whoosh though the wind will be beating there, the trees all crazy in Regent's Park, though closed its gates in the growing dark and the yelping wind your feet will take you where there's an opening in the fence, and going in your feet and Mirabel's will dare one another who can proceed faster down the curving path and leap over the little iron hoops on the edge of a turned up flower-bed, and reach the spot prepared there by centuries of weather and climate changes, now tropically dense and now ice-age bald, but for twelve or fifteen minutes between the eternal before and the eternal after yours this patch of earth where you will throw your trench coat and make it your bed and Mirabel will take two steps here and two steps there, doing a tribal dance while removing her tweed coat as if it were a bridal robe, and what ages come and what ages go, this will be the now, Mirabel pulling you down to the earth and flinging her coat over your back.

IV

What seest thou else
In the dark backward and abysm of time?

William Shakespeare, *The Tempest.*

AND THEN, WHEN all's done, and as in the mind of a drunk who's convinced he's newly acquired a comprehensive knowledge that makes him supremely enlightened about all considerations pertaining to life and death, you're persuaded that you've captured the beginning and the end, successfully chased away all intrusive shadows that make an unexpected appearance, as at the air terminal when, walking to the gate for your flight, you suddenly see a woman with remarkably exceptional features—her face and figure quite unrelated to your conception of beauty or to an idea of exotic loveliness but so stunningly unique that emotions erupt within you of longing, desire and an inexplicable remorse, for her image provokes a suggestive doubt at the back of your mind that there might be an error in your theory of aesthetics which you had presumed to have been flawless—who walks past you taking urgent strides towards a destination which you know will never be yours, but the last shadow chased away, you barely enjoy a moment's glimpse like that of a brightly lit landscape seen from a fast train when, as if the train went hurtling into a tunnel, the darkness of another shadow collapses upon you, confounding the beginning and the end, for in the fast train in the long tunnel you can't tell whether you're hurtling forwards or backwards or are not entirely still as in the centre of an endlessly revolving circle. What composed that landscape, the horizon curtained by poplars, was it, the white blossoms, if it was May in England, hawthorn surely, spilling over the fences, and the horse chestnuts too, white-white blossoms against the sudden everywhere-green of spring, sunlight falling on the couple-coloured fields where dappled cows loitered, quickly the world slipped past your eyes, that flaming red that burst into your vision then, no sunset smear on the horizon that but a copse of flame trees, a projection from the tropics, what were you looking at. No use asking. There's no question to answer. Ceaselessly the planets orbit in your dreamless night, your consciousness become a vapour, the body bound in the infinite space of a nutshell, and then where are you and where indeed is the universe, for imagine, out there, on the supposed, not the real, for there can be no reality where there are no dreams, but the supposed, admit it, the supposed ceaseless orbiting that had begun before there could be any human conception of a beginning and which you therefore presume will continue beyond any notion you can have of an ending, who can deny such logic, and you are there in that turning and turning, the whoosh whoosh whoosh that goes on in infinite space, enclosed though it may be in a nutshell, and therefore you too, you too, imagine that, you too, are in the programmed gyrations, turning and turning, a bit of planetary dust, the self that's but an astronomer's eye witnessing the shocking revelations of a celestial drama, and where are you then. No use asking. There's no question to answer. But look down and there's the classroom globe spun by a child's finger and then arbitrarily stopped, for why let the blur of blue oceans and green yellow and red land masses go round and round forever, the finger pokes a dot, and the polka-dotted universe halts over London, you're losing altitude rapidly, piercing the ceiling of clouds, falling through drifting banks of grey, seeing glimpses of buildings and green common land and the dark line of the river, and it's as if there were indeed a classroom in which your consciousness walked up and down the aisles like a schoolmaster observing the little heads of studious memories bent over their little exercise books in confessional solemnity, writing down what they've learned by rote, and you floated in the air over London, there in that suspended dust that never settles on the ground. Among weary-eyed school children impatient for the four o' clock bell, in Ealing, say, or in Hackney Wick, shoulders drooped in the late afternoon dolour, the schoolmaster lets the waves of chatter wash over his gravelly brain, now rushing in with a sudden surge and then going out with a sucking hiss, the momentarily uncovered fringe of broken shells in the lacey water like foam on the lip of a pint of ale, ceaseless

the coming and going, turning up some new fragment
that one barely identifies before it's sucked into the
depth or lost in the camouflage of the pebbly debris on
the water's edge. Why do you demand once more, what's
it all about then. No use asking. There's no question to
answer. Just foam on the pint of ale, drink up. Tumblers
and acrobats, Londoners, trapeze artists and fire-eaters,
buglers and trumpeters in the city's brassy cacophony.
More brown faces than last year among the pink, for the
empire has folded in upon itself, the periphery has
arched over and collapsed within the centre, more has
followed Clive's homeward bound baggage than diamonds, dark eyes apprehensive and curious on the brown
faces, where are we, where have we come from, is that
not the unexpressed thought behind the dark brown
eyes, and if that event of the journey, only that, the
departure and the arrival from one harbour or air terminal to another, were to be rehearsed completely again,
imagine only that, but even let that go unthought, don't
even think of what, thinking, will make you conclude
the thought wasn't worth puzzling over, and forget this
kind of smart circularity too, for is it not a prevarication,
this analysis, an avoidance, even a total suppression, of
what's easily remembered, is it not. No use asking.
There's no question to answer. Nice abstraction that, like
nothing but blue on an Yves Klein canvas, or *circularity,
prevarication, suppression*, like Rothko's triple bands, the
horizontal flow of colour, the impression of an idea

when it can't be expressed, impressive the flow of sound, the mind, in the end, as at the beginning, staring in amazement at a void and insisting there's a streak of yellow in the brown so dark it's black, a glimmer of red too in the black so fluid at the back of one's eyes it's the nearly black dark brown of flowing lava, or that moment between two notes, that pause which, however infinites-imal, is a prolonged silence, wet earth heaped on a road-side after a landslide entering one's vision as an imagined scrap, tiny points of light in that mass of wet earth, deep as the earth their meaning, those impressive words, what words. No use asking. There's no question to answer. Not long since you were the only brown in a classroom of thirty pink, that's not forgotten, is it. Even after *Max Simon* had substituted *Maqsood Zaman* and eliminated an offending foreign element from his English con-sciousness, Mr Watson still considered you a curiosity and distributing the parts of *Julius Caesar* for the only way he knew of teaching Shakespeare, making the class read him aloud while he himself looked at the ceiling, said, 'You be the Soothsayer, Simon, you Indians are fond of fortune-telling', that's not forgotten, is it. But then, marking essays one evening while the mother he lived with in a little terraced house in Fulham made his tea, Mr Watson looked up from the exercise book with the neat handwriting, removed his spectacles and rubbed his eyes, convinced that they must be tired and seeing things, but when he had rested his eyes for a minute and put on his glasses again, the word was still there: *oneiro-mancy*—spelling: correct; usage: precise, the sentence necessary to the essay's succession of ideas and not a superfluous insertion to create an opportunity to show off one's superior vocabulary, and what's more, a sentence that's expressive of a subtle reading of 'Kubla Khan'; Mr Watson again paused in his reading, placing a finger on the page he flipped back the cover, saw on it the name *Maqsood Zaman* and beneath it in brackets *Max Simon*, opened the exercise book as before, read the sentence again, leaned back, removed his glasses once more and stared at the ceiling; a little giggle escaped from his throat, for the thought associated with the poem—the glee with which boys each year recited the line, 'As if this earth in fast thick pants were breathing'— inevitably came to his mind, but suppressing the intrusive and irreverent thought, he reflected on the Indian boy's thinking and expression with a stunned sort of astonishment; his head still thrown back and his eyes still at the ceiling, a second association now cast its image on his mental screen—a voluptuous, plump-shouldered and round-breasted belly-dancer, her dark brown hair swirling around her head and her gold-trimmed long skirt swirling round her legs—an image that invariably sprang up in his mind in accompaniment of his recitation of his favourite line from the poem, 'A damsel with a dulcimer', which he always felt compelled to speak aloud when he remembered the poem; and just as he did

so and smiled, continuing to see the belly-dancing damsel on the ceiling, he heard a voice say, 'Charles, are you
all right?', and looked to see his mother standing in the
doorway with the tea tray in her hands and staring at
him, obviously alarmed at his condition. 'Dreams,
mother, dreams that are our bliss and our torment,' he
answered, 'who can divine dreams?' '*Charles . . . ,*' she
said in a tone of voice he had heard her use ever since
he was a child whenever she needed to reprimand him,
'. . . really!' Observing no change in his demeanour but
that a silly sort of grin remained fixed on his face, she
turned around to the kitchen, saying, 'Marmite will be
better for you than cherry jam'. Mr Watson made no
comment when he returned the essays to the class but
merely called out the boys' names and handed each back
his exercise book; a day later, however, when the class
resumed reading *Julius Caesar* and it was found that the
boy who had been assigned the part of Messala was
absent, Mr Watson cast his eyes across the classroom,
fixed them on Max and said, 'Simon, why don't you take
Messala?' It was the final act of the play and ten minutes
still remained of the period after the reading ended. The
class would next read *Antony and Cleopatra*, Mr Watson
announced, and gave out the parts. Knowing the play,
Max anticipated that he would again read the
Soothsayer's part and was mildly consoled by the
thought that the Soothsayer in *Antony* had several more
lines than the one in *Caesar*; instead he heard Mr Watson

say, 'Simon, you take Enobarbus'. When Mr Watson
assigned an essay on Browning's dramatic monologues
the next week in the literature class, Max produced a
paper that made an even greater impression on the
school master than had his earlier work that had alerted
Mr Watson to his brilliance; the teacher returned the
work without making a comment but when Max had
read aloud the dying speech of Enobarbus in the
Shakespeare class, Mr Watson held up his hand before
the next speaker could proceed in the reading, repeated
the famous line from Enobarbus's speech—'O sovereign
mistress of true melancholy'—said what a lovely line it
was and asked Max to read the speech again; and thus
was established a tacit practice between them by which
Mr Watson conveyed his high praise for Max's work
without alluding to it but by making him one of the
leading principals in any current project and Max
acknowledged the implied praise and thanked him by
producing a succession of essays with each one of which
he tried to exceed his previous accomplishment. At the
end of the summer term, Mr Watson asked Max to wait
a minute after the class had been dismissed. 'Let me lend
you this for the holidays,' he said, handing Max a book,
and Max, taking it and glancing at its spine where he
read LONGINUS *On the Sublime*, said, 'Have a good hol-
iday, sir'. To be noticed no longer as the conspicuous
brown mark among the pink faces but only acknowledged discreetly as a superior intelligence, a quiet

satisfaction that, that's not forgotten, is it. No use asking. There's no question to answer. Freer he was in that London, the thrill of English words so pumped his heart, roaming the heaths and the parks in blustery weather, wandering among the deserted streets of the City on Sunday mornings, loitering along the Embankment from Millbank to Chelsea, eyes incredulous that they gazed at the Thames which he had first seen in a Bombay classroom as the stressed syllable in an iambic foot. Incredible, too, in the Northern Line to Waterloo that the Tube ran under the river, flowed above his head the Thames, knocking at high tide the green-black stone of the embankment below Cleopatra's Needle. Peculiarly different from point to point the sensation of underground London, he could tell, not taking his eyes off the book in his hands, *There is sweet music here that softer falls*, from the sound of the wheels as the Piccadilly Line slowed and turned and then straightened and accelerated that the train was between South Ken and Knightsbridge or when there was a slight suppression of the echo that the tube had narrowed and the commencement of the fast run, his eyes still on the book, *But, propt on beds of amaranth and moly*, meant that the train was about to speed between King's Cross and Caledonian Road, after which, at Holloway Road, he must alight, just over a page of the poem left, time enough to finish it, *To watch the long bright river drawing slowly*, before he got off, the book a Penguin that fit neatly in the left pocket of his coat. THE

Penguin Poets *The Centuries' Poetry* 4 Hood to Hardy One shilling and sixpence. The fast run's coming to an end. Pocket the book. Hardy. Far from the madding crowd two on a tower the return of the native Jude the Obscure Tess. *He hears it not now, but used to notice such things.* Holloway Road. Come up from the underground. Grace in her flat off Holloway Road, her mother gone away at last, rosebud pink walls in her small bedroom, bed of amaranth and moly, tightly clinging her arms, and pink-polished her nails on her long fingers, Grace, the ageless older woman whose lips whispered magical charms that mocked appearances and transformed the boy to a lover encaged in her long arms. First on Box Hill in Surrey, then in Epping Forest in Essex, then in Kew and then Parliament Hill Fields, green the circle through which she drew him and under oaks and chestnuts and among ferny groves whispered charms, round and round on heath and parkland the circle tightened towards London's centre where inside the vast hollow trunk of a tree in Hyde Park her whispering pierced his ear-drum and possessed his brain as in an ecstatic conclusion to some pagan ritual. Bright her eyes in the face he held that looked up at him, knowledge there of his blood. Green that London, winter or summer, rain or sun, glowed her eyes when they saw the boy possessed. Up from the Tube, up from London's depth. Around the corner from Holloway Road. Even in the deep, the Piccadilly Line speeding smoothly from King's Cross, his eyes fixed on the page, *Music that gentlier on the spirit lies*, there was a backdrop of green as if Grace had him pressed to the ground and over her shoulder he saw the tossing branches of an elm. Around the corner, ageless older woman, a little meal prepared for him, devilled eggs, lamb cutlets, on a little table covered with a baby blue cloth, a peeled peach soaked in a liqueur, a worshipper's little magical offerings made from sacred ingredients, pagan prayers upon her painted lips, brightly wide her eyes that watched him with a devotee's fervent hope and expectation, up from the underground, round the corner. Some potion thus making his optic nerve throb, he saw her body in mottled light, the white skin smoother because bordered by dark shadow like a sand dune upon which angled light makes the grainy white appear smooth and white and the shadow across the slope a solid matt black and he nuzzled against her dappled breast, caught in the embrace of the ageless woman who from eternity had not altered and whose charm would be infinite, sweet birds in her vocal chords that sang to him. But then one day as if he stood in a desert in the midday sun, the light was without magic, only a bright glare, coarse sand only where no shadow fell, porous and grainy her skin, narrow the ravine of time that trapped her, no nightingale there but a smoker's rattle and phlegm in her throat, old the older woman. Around the corner, down, down the lift, deep in tunnelled London, HOOD TO HARDY again open, *Was a lady such a lady, cheeks so round and lips so red*—no use asking, there's no question to answer, Galuppi at the clavichord in Venice, the masked revellers scarcely hearing his cold music, *Dust and ashes, dead and done with*, trapped in that ravine. Fled from that trap the cruel youth, slipped out of her snakeskin arms, plugged his ears against her love-and-marriage song. At Hyde Park he came up from the underground, felt the wind in his hair and numbingly cold on his skin, a liberating cold as if it would be happiness to bare one's breast and make keener its penetration there, and he took long, jaunty strides along the Serpentine, walking past empty rowing boats that rocked on the agitated water's edge. He did not look to the right where in a little grove that tree was with its enormous hollow trunk where Grace had taken him by the hand and led him as into some sacred grotto, ageless female form then, Grace, ancient the deep craving within her womb, and he did not wish to look where he had entered, blindly. He walked past the rocking boats, keeping his eyes on the disturbed water. Dust and ashes, dead and done with, the cruelty of time one could say if pushed to rush into a cliché by the absurdity of vanity, but in all reality one cannot, for were he to look at the tree, he would still be there and Grace with her cheek on his thigh, the throbbing moment still throbbing, the tension of what's to come still suspended, what cruelty then, what time, no use asking, there's no question to answer. The wind felt sharper when he stood on the bridge. Flag flying over Westminster, low the torn and ragged clouds flying confusedly as if the wind constantly changed direction, a commotion in the trees that looked like flocks of birds were restlessly fluttering there, the wind whistled through the branches, tearing leaves. He looked down on the turbulent water. One boat there, rising and falling among the waves, a dark-haired young man in a brown suit straining at the oars, the collar of his double-breasted jacket turned up against the wind, a girl opposite him crouching with her head bent low and touching her drawn-up knees where a scarlet tartan skirt is stretched taut, the wind sweeping over her back. Max turned around and walked towards Kensington Gardens. Albert all golden now, a gleaming monument for point-and-shoot tourists. A number 9 double-decker to Aldwych on Kensington Road across from Albert, its dark-skinned driver vaguely staring at the passes of the boarding old-age pensioners. Wind cold in the Flower Walk. Max, Max said to himself, where are you, Max. He was there, though no blooms now on the rhododendrons, with Jenny, surely that depression in the earth, no one has stepped on it, whose that form if not hers. Colder outside the Flower Walk. Red-eyed with hay-fever, Mirabel, whose that sneezing if not hers. Max, where are you. No use asking. There's no question to answer. A sudden boom as of thunder but the sound that followed he recognized as the four loudly revving engines of a Boeing 707 and looking up he saw shadowy glimpses of

it among the billows of fast-moving clouds and then suddenly it appeared in a momentary opening between the
racing clouds, loud in its descent as it came down from
the north and banked over the river and aimed west for
Heathrow, using the power of its four engines to reduce
the buffeting wind to rolling level steady air, lit up in
golden streaks where the sun's rays hit its breast, and
then with an accelerating thrust off forth it swung and
plunged into a cloud to emerge lower and now so lit by
the full sun it seemed on fire, lovely and dangerous the
gold-vermilion flames that broke from its wings. *O my
chevalier!* But it did not descend, held instead its height
and commenced a banking circle over the city, the starboard wing pointing to the earth: yours the eyes at the
window just in front of the wing, the terraced and
semi-detached suburbs spin round and disappear behind
a low cloud, the sun cuts through the cloud and suddenly shines over green land, your eyes ablaze now looking down on that melodious plot of beechen green, and
there under the green ascent of sycamores is the shadow-self almost indistinguishable from shadows that
numberless fall in the grove, tight the circle of this flight,
vanished the clouds and the sun now pours molten gold
over the parks, from Hampstead Heath you swoop over
Regent's Park in that tight banking curve, and there,
almost over the river but still the starboard wing tilted
towards the earth, you glide past Hyde Park and
Kensington Gardens, and now the plane should surely

swing back and follow the river for its final descent to
Heathrow, but it continues its wide, banking curve in
the same holding pattern, and again you're over
Hampstead and then again over Kensington, and once
more and then once more, the sun's gold now a ring
encircling the parks whose green fringed with gold looks
a deeper green, deeply all that you love embedded in
that many-layered green, and there slips the shadow-self
into the green so green its black silhouette's absorbed into
the green heart of London, once more and then once
more, you lean away from the window, for a moment
close your eyes and as in the mirror in which appeared
the eighth king you see appear and dissolve a succession
of soft-focus portraits where before you begin to recog-
nise Grace you believe it's Brenda but no sooner she than
Jenny and before you can say her name it's Mirabel but
she too dissolves and gives way to the one nameless, in
this eternal circling, once more and then once more, you
lean forward again and for a moment believe the window
to be a mirror filled with her face, whose, no use asking,
hers, once more and then once more what else can you
see but London's green, there's no question to answer, the
light golden in her green eyes, whose, hers, but then you
see the reflection is from two pools, there's only the green
of London into which dissolve the succession of portraits
and the fugitive shadow-self slips over the green as if the
sun projected the plane's shadow on the swaying tops of
the elms, the birches, the chestnuts, the oaks.

CPSIA information can be obtained
at www.ICGtesting.com
Printed in the USA
BVHW090945190920
589090BV00005B/15